THE AUTHOR

RAYMOND KNISTER was born in Ruscom, Ontario, in 1899. He enrolled in Victoria College, University of Toronto, in 1919, but contracted pneumonia and was forced to withdraw. From 1920 until 1923 he continued writing and studying on his own while working on his father's farm near Blenheim, Ontario. In 1923 he went to Iowa City for a year as one of the associate editors of *The Midland*, an avant-garde literary magazine; he also took some courses in creative writing at the University of Iowa. He returned to Canada in 1924 to help his father move to a new farm. In 1926 he moved to Toronto to embark on a full-time writing career.

In the eleven years from his first short story in 1921 until his drowning in 1932, Knister wrote three novels set in Ontario; a non-fiction novel, *My Star Predominant*, based on the life of John Keats; nearly one hundred short stories; about the same number of poems; and a play. In addition to count-less book reviews and articles, he also edited *Canadian Short Stories* (1928), the first anthology of Canadian short fiction.

White Narcissus, published in 1929 in Canada, England, and the United States, was the only novel Knister published in his lifetime.

Raymond Knister drowned off Stoney Point, Ontario, in 1932.

WHITE NARCISSUS

RAYMOND KNISTER

AFTERWORD BY
MORLEY CALLAGHAN

First published in 1929 by Macmillan of Canada
New Canadian Library edition copyright © Canada, 1962 by
McClelland and Stewart Limited

Afterword copyright © 1990 by Morley Callaghan

Reprinted 1990.
This New Canadian Library edition 2010.

Library and Archives Canada Cataloguing in Publication

Knister, Raymond, 1899-1932
      White narcissus / Raymond Knister ; afterword by Morley Callaghan.

(New Canadian library)
ISBN 978-0-7710-9402-6

      I. Title. II. Series: New Canadian library

PS8521.N75W4 2010   c813'.52   C2010-900040-4

We acknowledge the financial support of the Government of Canada
through the Book Publishing Industry Development Program and that of
the Government of Ontario through the Ontario Media Development
Corporation's Ontario Book Initiative. We further acknowledge the support
of the Canada Council for the Arts and the Ontario Arts Council for our
publishing program.

Typeset in Garamond by M&S, Toronto
Printed and bound in Canada

ANCIENT FOREST
FRIENDLY

McClelland & Stewart Ltd.
75 Sherbourne Street
Toronto, Ontario
M5A 2P9
www.mcclelland.com/NCL

1 2 3 4 5   14 13 12 11 10

For Myrtle

Feelings and unwisdom make all men kin.

FRIEDERICH FRESKA

ONE

Richard Milne was only two hours away from the
city, and it seemed to be still with him. He found
incredibly foreign the road down which he swung,
as though with resolution. Its emptiness shortly became
impressive. He met no one, and it seemed to lead burrow-
ing, dusty, into the bleak wind, into the centre of lost wastes
screened by scattered and fretful trees. The trees sighed as
though in abandonment from struggling forests which, the
man knew, would seem to recede as he went forward. He
felt lost in this too-familiar country, and slackened his pace.

It was an immediate relief to get out of Lower Warping
after ten minutes tramping its empty and shrunken streets,
and inquire for a lodging-place. The old Hotel, known to his
boyhood by no other name – blue-grey clapboards, two
storeys and gable windows breasting the cross-roads – was
closed. Richard Milne saw that before he had gone a hundred
yards down the cindered path from the station. He went back
to learn from a meditative youth on a baggage truck whether
there was now any other hotel in the place.

"Nope!" The fellow's grin showed a gap in his teeth. He raised his voice against an irruption of the departed, hooting train. "Tom Hughes puts up the travellers sometimes. If you're travellin' with some line he buys, you might try there. He lives above the store. Was you going to stay long?"

Prohibition, it appeared, had caused the place to close, at which Milne was inclined to wonder, since it had afforded hospitality to his last visit, scarcely a year ago. In any event, the remainder of the hamlet was so torpid that on the spur of the moment he determined to get out of it at once, and without seeking a welcome from any of these people who, it came to him, must exist, for the flowers beside their coloured verandas twitched peevish, proud heads in the wind, while the wire gates before their lawns were primly closed. And if he succeeded in finding them, would anyone remember him? No, he would walk out to the farm. For some reason he did not leave his bag, but carried it in his hand.

This matter was only one in the series of actions and adjustments which were a part of his determination, of his plans, and of the trip from the city. He had passed through it all with the impulsive consciousness of nothing but the goal. He must see Ada Lethen, though it were for the last time. Now, alone on the windy road, he began to hesitate, to wonder. The fields, river banks, the astounding, overwhelming sky he seemed to have forgotten, questioned him as an alien. What was he doing there? And what good, he further asked himself, would his coming do? He had returned often enough before. He was moved to ward off despair by reminding himself that he could do nothing else. He had been compelled to come back. But if memory could prove so fugacious, how had he trusted it so long? Uncertainty came into his mind. But lifting his head he went forward.

Like the village which had seemed still smaller than a village, smaller than it had ever been before, this countryside had the look of having arisen about him foreignly with the incredible immediacy of a dream. The road made fitful efforts at directness, and would ignore the swing of the high river-banks, only a little farther on to skirt a depression, a sunken, rich flat, bearing rank, blue-green oats surrounded by droop-ing willows, elms through which only a glimpse of the brown ripples of water could be seen; again, underbrush, small maples, wild apples, green sumach came right to the road and hung over the fence, hiding the drop of a ravine. A place of choked vistas.

The road was easy walking for the greater part, with firm gravel at first, and then, after a mile, occasional sandy spots, rutted, with hoof-beaten soil between the wheel marks. Richard Milne had buried his bare toes in this sand as a schoolboy. Recalling himself with a smile, he reflected that he was no longer much of a countryman, since he was allowing mere impressions of the place to take his mind, his eye, from its utilitarian aspect. He could not have told yet "how the crops looked," compared with the country he had seen from the train. And doubtless he would be asked by the first acquaintance he met to deliver an opinion.

Passably flourishing, he surmised, almost having forgot-ten how far these harvests, so assiduously watched over by men, should have progressed in maturity at the end of June. The corn, he recalled, should be knee-high by the twelfth of July, and was far from that now. The wheat was in head, though still green, short and spindly, waving on almost dis-cernible soil of light-coloured knolls. Oats were dark in the rich hollows, fading to a brighter green on the slopes. The clover heads were red, clustered; ah, there was something on which he could compliment an old-time friend. Perhaps the other things would come on better later.

He wasn't sure that he cared, he admitted, after these years. He had borne his share of such preoccupations, which seemed designed to pen his youthful hopes forever within this congeries of haphazard mis-shapen fields. Yet it all came back to him, fields and years, more poignant at every yard he traversed, and he knew that he could never be freed from the hold of this soil, however far from it he had travelled, though he were never to be called back by itself, but by a forfeit of love which in final desperation he had come to redeem or tear from its roots forever.

Again he found that he had hastened; then sauntering on with an appearance of ease, the memories stirred within him so that he should not have wished to meet an old neighbour on the road. Nothing could be farther from his wishes than a revealing sign of these conflicting emotions. At best it would be inadequate. And the presence of another would make any such display ridiculous, he reflected, thinking of the rebellious period in which he nearly had hated the place and its inhabitants. He glanced at the house he was passing.

Until now buildings had been part of the village in his mind and, indeed, there had been no rural mail-box at the roadside before this one. Lilac bushes stood at either side of the gate; a path curved from townward between the gate and across the lawn, long grass of an evenness which showed that occasionally it was mown. The lumbering farm-house seemed to stand on the edge of a brink, for nothing showed behind it but, in the distance, the round tops of apple trees, grey-green in the almost apparent wind. At the first glance he felt that the barn and other buildings might have dropped away, but turning he saw the unpainted, sagging-ridged building standing on the edge of the hollow, as near the road where he had unwittingly passed it, as the house. It had been moved up from the slope behind in his absence.

He knew this place very well, but not these improvements. It was the farm his uncle had owned, where he had lived as a boy. As he passed he looked at the mail-box. William A. Burnstile was the name. . . . How? Raffish, turbulent Bill Burnstile, big boy of the country school, up to whom little Dick Milne had looked with the hero-worship only bad boys can evoke – chronically unstable on growing up, until his departure for "the West" – was Bill Burnstile the firmly-established, evidently prudent or lucky farmer of this place?

While Richard Milne meditated, wondering whether he could not satisfy his curiosity as well as his need by putting up here for the night, he was decided by a series of shouts, wails, and pursuing cries. A boy of eleven with yellow hair on a thin neck rushed around the corner of the house, followed by a series younger, and turned at bay against their tumbling charge. Obviously this was no place for his sojourning; still, fascinated, he stayed and watched the children. The first, with exultant yips, trotted in a circle, and held high above his head a kitten, which clawed wistfully for a footing on the air. Two smaller boys, with shouts, jumped to reach it, seized the other by the legs and downed him to his own deprecating yells of "No fair, le' me 'lone." While they wrestled and squirmed in the grass, a little girl approached, and stepping gingerly among legs, managed to get hold of the kitten. She was running toward the man, to hide behind the snowball bushes at the side of the lawn, when an older girl appeared, calling out to the others. At that instant both girls caught sight of the stranger, and a hush came over the whole serried group of children, puffing yet with their struggle.

For an instant Richard Milne did not know whether or not to pass on. Of course, he would not stay here by deliberate choice, even if he could be accommodated. Still, there was his curiosity. "Boys!" he called. "Is this where Mr. Burnstile lives?"

They nudged each other to go and see what the man wanted. Finally, the second boy, the doughty wrestler, left the others and came over to the fence, turning his head in the wind as though to listen, his yellow hair ruffling. "Can't hear. Wind's wrong way."

"Is this where Mr. Burnstile lives? I mean, ah, Bill Burnstile?"

"Why, that's me! Oh, you mean my dad. Yes, he lives here. He's cutting hay. Will any of us do?"

The man smiled. "Yes. Your father was out West for a time, wasn't he? Well, you tell him that Dick Milne was here. Just see if he remembers."

"Ouch! That's Poison Ivy." The boy had been leaning too close to the fence. "What? Oh, all right. I'll tell him." With a last look of wonder at the clothes of the stranger he was gone, skipping into the midst of the other children, who in the meantime had approached nearer – like steam melting into a cloud. The girl with the forgotten cat dangling looked after him.

They were so like a little group of perturbed animals, crying out half-audibly there in the wind, that Richard Milne laughed as he went on. The sight of the country children strangely refreshed him, and no longer was the place alien, but lonesome, waiting to welcome the footsteps of any returning wanderer. He smiled. This life was all as it had been, though these boys and girls would lack the excitement of his own childhood in recognizing "an old tramp."

Evening was coming on, and even the apparently endless stationary evening of June waned after the supper hour. That consideration at least should urge him forward. Again he wondered; it seemed strange that no one he knew appeared in these familiar spaces. There was, of course, the one unchanging farm, where all his hopes were centred, his ultimate destination, and where he could expect no welcome. But surely before reaching it he would find people less interested in himself. He would have no trouble about a place for the night, and somewhere, if needed, there would be a boarding place for longer. He had money, after all, and that was usually unfailing in incidental uses. Still, the club-bag was becoming notably heavy.

The land became more rolling, hummocky, confused, with bare cultivated spots, thick brush along random, half-concealed fences. The road and the river seemed to rival each other in the vagrancy of their courses. The banks were now white clay, now green with weedy grass or up-grown shrubbery, a brief row of tall trees – over all of which the sun flowed coldly. A man was tiny enough in the midst of great cities, he remembered strangely, but here it was possible to wonder how many more of these roads there were stretching away into the evening, endlessly, bearing each its strung-out farms, its weight of enigmatic human and animal circumstance.

He seemed suddenly to have walked a great distance. A burden of his own past seemed to have descended upon him. How beautiful all this had been, and as the years of his boyhood slipped past without more than a dream of wider freedom, how dreary! The changing of the seasons had only emphasized the impression of monotony, and he had been held by inertia, and uncertain hope of fulfilment, on the only soil he knew. He had begun to write, and it was comparatively late that he had obeyed that questing-spirit which is the heritage of youth. Well, he had gone into the world and done all that he had dreamed of doing, and he had returned frequently enough with the one purpose, to the one being which could call him back; and still the land was the same, with a sorrowful sameness. It seemed that the beauty of this country should have increased, become clear and undeniable even to its preoccupied inhabitants. It always seemed that these people should have found larger interest and a wider view during his own period of Wanderjahre and Lehrjahre.

But now he was coming to the Hymerson farm. Here he knew he would be safe, more or less at home. Old friends of his family in a large phrase, old neighbours at least, they would be glad to see him, if only from curiosity. There did not seem to be improvements in the place, he noted, nor neglect. Wire fencing extending part way along the road, then the old rankly growing hedge, until that was clipped low in front of the house. This was a great affair of cheap yellow brick, which had been a show-place in his boyhood. It already showed signs of decay. The roof, of wooden shingles, was brown, the wood of the gables stained brown with weather, and the originally white veranda posts and scrollings were flaked grey and lead-coloured. There were high weeds along the roadside, and the lawn itself was lush with grass, except for spots uprooted in irregular holes. The source of these holes became apparent in squeals from behind the house. The chorus, kept up so pertinaciously, foretold the supper hour of the pigs.

Entering in at the open lane, for there was no gate to the lawn, Richard Milne saw again the familiar buildings. The barn, an L-shaped huge structure of splotched grey beneath an old coat of pink paint, had been raised upon a foundation of cement blocks, abutted by lengthy graded approaches, which occupied much of the space of the yard.

The yard was a broad expanse strewn with apparent indiscrimination: smaller buildings and used machinery. A long, slatted corn-crib with sway-back roof looked as though, empty, it could have been drawn away by a team of horses. But yellow ears of corn protruded between the slats at one end, a remainder after the winter's feeding. A similarly disreputable granary stood at the other side. And all about sprawled culti-vators, harrows, discs, a mower, a bare wagon, the rack of which leaned against the side of the corn-crib.

These machines were not rusted in any state of disuse. In fact, they and the buildings, instead of giving the place a general effect of neglect, imparted a business-like aspect, as of work being in progress which forbade such fol-de-rols as neatness, newness, paint, and shelter from the elements of air and earth, for which all things were, in any case, ultimately destined.

Before Richard Milne came to the house he saw crossing the yard in the rear a flapping, overalled, small figure of a man, carrying a pair of dripping swill-pails. He waved, going forward without setting down his club-bag. It was Carson Hymerson, who went on to the swill-barrels and dipped the pails, heaving them out with a swish of water whitened by the admixture of chopped grain, and vegetable refuse curling over the rims.

"Just time supper, have good trip out? Hogs here they know it's time for supper, 'Spose you're glad to get away to the country once 'nawhile, how long you goin' to stay?" Hymerson said all this apparently without breath, and with the auto-matic and evenly timed swiftness of a phonographic record turned at twice its normal speed. It was just his way, Richard remembered people said, as he shook hands with him. The farmer was over fifty, but still his ruddy, hard face, tinged to brass colour by tan, was unchanged by wrinkles, knobby as ever as to chin, nose, cheek-bones, and saltily blue of eye. "Well, Missus'll want to see you better go in supper, I'll be there right now."

Milne hesitated, still holding his bag, but the tone had been so arbitrary that, considering that the man might have some other immediate task before the meal, he turned back toward the house, walking over a series of long, warped boards under the edges of which grass grew. The surface of the yard was sparsely green in places, where vegetation had survived the trampling of mud in the spring.

The screen-door under the porch was open, a wood-burning range hummed cheerily, and there were steps from another room. "Shoo! Scat out of here!" A black cat sped before her, but Mrs. Hymerson, compared with her husband, was ceremonial in her reception. She wore a white shirtwaist with high collar, and a black pleated skirt.

"Why, how do you do; you're quite a stranger, Richard. But I suppose I should call you Mr. Milne. I thought, you know, I heard Carson talking to somebody, but I couldn't just be sure. You must stay for tea. How's –" She seemed to recall that he lived apart from relatives, that he had no near ones. "How's everything in the city? It must be hot there! Well! It's nice to have you come back and see us." She nodded.

Richard Milne, in the polite replies permitted him at intervals, was conscious of a subdued reservation, like excitement coming unreasonably into his mind. It was impatience, he discovered. He wanted to cloak it in random conversation, discussion of country doings, anything. He could have tried to arrange some provision for a long stay, but he knew that Mrs. Hymerson would be offended if he immediately proposed a definite arrangement. And then his uncertainty recalled that he did not know himself how long or in what manner he would be staying.

TWO

He had washed the grime from hands and face in the kitchen, wiped on a prickly towel, and was sitting at the supper table where Mrs. Hymerson, who insisted that they should not wait, was pouring tea, before the farmer came in, breathing audibly. Calves from a neighbouring farm had broken through the line fence; he had seen them afar off browsing on his oats, and chased them.

"Well, we'll go and call on him after supper, you and I," he announced to Milne.

"Are they from the Lethen side?" asked the latter.

"Certainly they're from Lethen's. That old man's past farming, if he ever was any good at it. Can't even keep up his fences. Why he ever stays on — But then you must remember. Bet he'd seem as old when you were a kid as he does now."

"I remember how impressive he appeared, with his young brown face and his white hair. I hadn't seen anyone like him; and when I got to know him a little better he never quite became commonplace."

"Quite a character." Mrs. Hymerson smiled, as though she knew and wished to take the flavour from what her husband was about to express. "And you know, he knows more than you'd think, too. They say he was well educated when he was young. . . ."

"Appear distinguished, I guess he does, appear," burst in the rapid accents of Carson Hymerson. "That's all he does, is appear, the old fraud, don't I know him, know him like a book! I guess I ought to, hmph!" The man drew up his right shoulder and twisted his head aside in a grimace of cynic humour. "Why, when I and he was on the school-board, there never was any peace, but he'd be thinking up ideas. And you couldn't do anything with him, once he got an idea in his head. Crazy, that's what he is, crazy, and he don't know it." The last few swift words came in a lower tone, for he was not unaware of Richard Milne's reception of them, a hardening of the mouth.

"I am sorry to hear that. Mr. Lethen must have changed. It seemed to me that he was the kind of man who, if he could make out to live in the country at all, would be of invaluable service." The younger man spoke with a deliberation which spoke of long-weighed conclusions, and a disposition to regard only politeness in listening to whatever might be said on the subject. Carson Hymerson heard him with impatient snorts, scarcely able to keep from interrupting but, perhaps because of the still regard of his wife, less acrid in tone when he did rattle:

"You might think so. It's quite a while since you had much to do with old Lethen, ain't it? Well! You ask the neighbours when you want to find out about a man! You can ask. . . ." He mumbled, then went on with greater heat. "Invaluable use, why that's just what he ain't, is useful."

"Yes, of course, it must be kind of past his time for working very hard." Mrs. Hymerson, Richard Milne's amusement noted, had preserved a sense for affable adjustment which her husband might never have possessed. The latter was not going to let her smooth things over.

"Why, look at the way he's always lived with that woman of his. That's enough for me, never speaking! And take his daughter. . . ."

"Yes . . . ?" began Richard, so quickly that the woman at once struck in, high-pitched.

"All I say is . . . all I say is, we can't ever *know*, don't you see, what may be at the bottom of these things. Everyone has their cross to bear, and we can't always understand, so it behooves us not to judge others." Mrs. Hymerson's voice became more even as she went on, despite the snort of Carson, as though she were reciting a well-remembered scriptural lesson. Milne, too grateful now that a moment of rage had passed not to abet her irrelevance, turned to her.

"Is Arvin not at home now, Mrs. Hymerson? I hope you'll pardon my not inquiring before; I missed him at once, of course."

"Arvin, he went out in the country to-day to look for a cow. Kind of running out of good cows, some going dry, going to fat a couple for beef. So I thought I'd give the boy a chance, let him use his own head this time and buy one without me near. I hope he don't get beat," he added grimly.

Richard Milne could not forbear a smile, which only belatedly he reflected might be taken as derogatory to the young man, twenty-six at the time of his last visit, but schooled – better, dragooned – by his father's impatience daily.

"That's fine." The remark hearty and sincere. "I don't think they'll get ahead of Arvin in a deal."

"And how is your – work progressing?" asked Mrs. Hymerson, beaming. "I've heard a lot about your books.

They happen around here. Two of them, you've written, haven't you?"

Three had been published, Richard told her. "Things are going well enough that I'm taking a holiday." He chuckled. "Keeping in the office, where most of my work with the advertising agency is done, gets pretty tiresome, especially at this season of the year."

"Get you fellows out in the hayfield," was Hymerson's jocular amenity. "Find out it was hot enough there, too."

The young man did not reply to this, reflecting almost with dismay that he had forgotten the terms of intercourse in the country, by which it was necessary that he should be able to "give as good as was sent." Doing that, in fact, was one of the chief roads to respect – one certainly blocked to him, even if the restraint caused him to appear morose.

"Our work," he proceeded, "is interesting; so we are told by people who don't know it. And certainly it has a fascination. It's fun to know that you are writing for a million readers, from the start." This was a rough effort at approximation to which he felt that a response could be sought. Nothing tried him more than talking of his good work, his creative books, to curious or indifferent people, and he valued the topic of advertising in proportion to the lack of immediacy it had for him. From the time of his rural upbringing he retained a sense that no one but other craftsmen really could be concerned in such matters.

He listened idly to the exclamations of his hostess and the dubious questions of Carson Hymerson really in swelling restiveness. He fancied that the shadow of the cross-piece of the screen-door crept across the kitchen floor with a surreptitious spurt. The evening would be upon him.

The meal was finished, and he had relished the potatoes fried in butter, the cold boiled pork, homemade bread, and rhubarb sauce. Carson Hymerson was in no haste now to rise, but drank a third cup of tea. At a remark upon the return of Bill Burnstile with a family, he sucked his lips and said complacently:

"Yes, rolling stone, Bill. Expect he'll be pulling out of *here*, even, one of these times, eh? Yes, he did collect a family, all right. Guess his woman's a pretty fair woman to help get along too, or he wouldn't be able to make a payment on a place like he has." He made the pronouncement with an unwavering, as it were a significant gaze of the little blue eyes in the direction of his wife, and Richard Milne turned to her. He would have to look up Bill while he was here.

"All the old neighbours," she assented, while Carson rapidly demanded how long he intended to stay. "Most of them are here yet. Not many have moved away."

"A few days, perhaps longer," Richard said, with an assumption of certainty surprising to himself, adding, "I think I'll take a stroll down the road this evening."

Carson seemed to be replying to his wife. "Good riddance if some would get out, let their land be farmed right." A thought seemed to strike him. "You wouldn't be going to Lethen's to-night, would you?"

"Yes," agreed Richard Milne candidly. "I'll probably call there." He paid no more attention to the anxious, almost signalling look of the woman than Carson Hymerson himself did. The latter seemed to regard him with stupefaction, which merged into an awkward grin of mocking badinage.

"Oh, I see! There's attraction over there, come to think of it. Not that I blame you. Now that I remember, you did use to kind of shine around Ada when you was a young gaffer. That's all right!"

They had risen from the table by this time, and a slow-mounting annoyance approaching anger had modified Richard Milne's haste to get away. "That's pleasant," he asserted. He secured his hat and went outside, to the accompaniment of the housewife's expressed wish that he remember her to Mrs. Lethen; but Carson was still beside him, hands comfortably stuck in deep overall pockets.

"Kind of looks as though I wasn't going to have you help me see to them calves after all, eh? Unless you go that way through the fields with me. Maybe I'll see you over there, anyway. Ha! Ha! But, of course, you wouldn't be coming away with me yet so early. Well, I'll see the door's left unlocked for you."

Milne thanked him with a grave smile, as one willing to accept all this as well-intentioned jocosity, and hurried down the lane to the road. His chief feeling was one of haste.

"Well, don't go 'way mad, looks like it was going to freeze, don't it," was the parting sally, which his mind repeated to his hurried steps down the dry road.

THREE

The wind was dying before the sunset, but had chilled, turning up the under sides of leaves. Trees shivered under a dulled sky. The evening, muted by wind and cold, given a sullen swiftness of animation, mated the feeling of Richard Milne. After a week of torrid weather in which the very sky seemed to melt, rain should have come to sweeten the smell of ripening grain and whitened clods. But first this dry cold, in which trees writhed blanching, while now and again a cricket chirping up fitfully made still greater the removal from the sultry quietude proper to the time and season.

Once more the man was overcome by a sense of strangeness. He had been in his office that morning, had walked and taxied in the streets of the city and left it at noon, riding through unforgettable miles of railway yards and factories and grimy suburbs. And already he could make himself believe in the existence of such things only with an effort. For all the years in which he had struggled for success there, it seemed that the only real and personal part of his life had been lived here, surrounded by trees, fields, river, which claimed him as though he had never left them. He did not need to look at this house or hedge or vista for a landmark, because he could have believed that he had walked down this road every night for the past year. And accompanying the return upon him bodily of the old life was the same sense of futility and uncertainty which he had known in those times – the cause of his eventual determination to leave, and also of his periodic returns. And with every step he was approaching nearer the source of that uncertainty.

The Lethen place hid the sunset, looming beyond a dredged cut to the river, like a moat, dry and overgrown with weeds. The tangle of vegetation, which in this light seemed to overlay the buildings, was in itself a quickening token to Richard Milne's remembrance, and he slowed, paused. Great evergreens shadowed the front of the place and guided his footsteps toward the lane. Dust flurried about him impotently as he reached the little leaning gate and went across the front yard, itself no haven to him: a wild expanse of grass and pine needles shadowy and whispering to his rising excitement of insuperable awaiting barriers.

The house was old, its narrow windows peered dark from drapery of Virginia Creeper, only the gables showing the weathered brick expanse which towered remote as though to scan the oblivious invader below. There was something secret but secure about the air of the house, like an awareness of its life indecipherable in dark hiding of the vines. So much of its appearance Richard Milne knew more from an act of memory than by bodily sight. He had reached the low weathered wooden gate giving on the lawn, and he became unconscious of everything for that moment, of the mysteriously-quickened night, the house, the trees, the dark, the pressing sky. For he knew that Ada Lethen was on the veranda before him, a few steps before his feet.

Her white dress stirred against the dusk, and he was filled and enveloped, overwhelmed with sense of her. He surprised a look of gladness and incredulity on her pale face as she slowly rose to greet him. And as of old her nervous pale fingers fluttered to her hair.

"Richard Milne! Why are you here? When did you come?"

He held her hand, looking into her darkened eyes, almost level with his own. "You are asking!" he exclaimed slowly. "Do you know, I couldn't quite believe – well, in you." Suddenly he realized it. "Ever since I got off the train I've been hurried, urged by something. Something was wrong – at least; and I had to see you to believe that this sorry, this decorative and rapscallion world did hold you – all that you mean." In a boyish access he laughed.

She laughed a little, with an intonation of sadness, withdrawing her hand. "Sit down. You've not changed. When did you come?" She moved two books on the seat, and reposed beyond them.

He sighed, still lost in the sight of her. "Then you don't refuse to see me, you don't send me away this time . . . or not yet." His tone was reproachfully accusing, more than ironical. She smiled faintly. Her pale, almost sallow face had become radiant.

"Why shouldn't I be . . . simply enchanted, to see an old friend?" She spoke softly. "Not every evening. . . . It's a long time. . . ."

His mind refused to hope, to consider implications, overpowering, impossible and rapt. He was not annoyed by the word "friend." It was enough to be here. Without touching them he indicated the books.

"You still read a great deal." His tone strove to flit to a

lightness belying his pity, the feeling in his familiar recognition which had brought the tears to his eyes when he met her. "Still," he had said. And "not every evening" did he come.

He had long since for all his freedom in thought, his assent to her ideals, looked with uneasiness upon her unremitting, her almost possessed reading. That feeling was beyond his rationalizing. He had been able to object only interferingly, as he felt powerless. What were books to her? Anodyne, perhaps, and they had to be of increasing potency. She paid little heed to him. What was she to do? She had been too wise to put it so, knowing what his answer would be. He felt absurd to cavil, though he did not like some of the things she read. . . . In his remark was contained a whole cycle of reminiscence, of familiarity which now seemed impossible.

"Yes, the books." She spoke in tones which to his cherished vision of her were what finality is to despair. "I read a great deal still – still."

Her present listlessness did not relieve him, but incongruously made him more anxious for her. He tried to speak as casually as a stranger.

"I remember them, your wide and esoteric explorations! Am I to take it that you are wearying of wandering? Or are you only temporarily abashed by the illimitable wastes, you're waiting to start forth again, afresh – you see the minarets of your city, lost in vapour, and you pause; and its riddle, while you rest, calls again. Its riddle. . . ." As he went on, the words seemed to flow automatically, as though he were drunk with a surprise of enchantment, while he watched her happy and tired face.

"The riddle," she murmured. They were silent a little. "That alone used to serve as reward, but it is long since the penance."

"I am not a riddle, but a man," he reminded her. "Come, are you so quiet because you think I am a ghost? You want proof!" But he did not touch her. "I should inquire about your parents, the circumstances of your life which nobody else knows."

He had spoken as though determinedly gay, cheering one sick; and now there was purpose in the indirect reference to her family, as of a relic of embitterment.

Ada Lethen laughed. "Do I seem so quiet? I assure you it's not because I don't appreciate, in all the word means, that you are here. Only the other day Mother was speaking to me of you."

"Did she?"

His eagerness was based, again, upon imagined changes during his absence. But it was no time yet to stake anything on the possible discovery of what had taken place in that house. "I hope Mrs. Lethen has been in good health lately?"

"Not exactly. She never is, of course, that would be too much to expect. Lately at times she seems better, and then a day or a week will come when she alarms me." Though the voice was soft, her articulation was definite and precise, her manner quietly explanatory, so that Richard Milne at moments fancied he was in a dream, not there, that far away she, like himself, sat alone.

He saw the real image of her as she sat alone, while seasons passed. How else should she sit, though her reason for being in that house always had been to keep from loneliness the father and mother whose estrangement had been one of the legends of his childhood? In itself that was enough to make for loneliness, and he marvelled at her endurance, her poised good sense. With the coming of womanhood, should she not feel free? But she could not believe in freedom.

She was talking softly, with the same certainty in which she had always shaken her head at his reasonings, his pleadings, implying that he understood her situation better than he pretended.

And in reality that was the case. He understood, but he felt surely that if the pair had been left to themselves long ago, they probably long ago should have become reconciled. Yet what seemed reasonable and practicable in the daylit world of the material and of work, ebbed away from him here before the power of a reality long-accepted, which denied the existence of all else. And peering into the past to that child, strange-eyed, fearfully-watchful, wounded, which Ada Lethen must have been, he felt that her presence might have been a sword between the two, so that they could never forget the bitterness of the first few days after the quarrel. That bitterness, dying away to inanition, died to a complete disregard so deep that they did not care to separate, even would not have done so, perhaps, had the girl not been there.

Ada Lethen was silent now, looking across the fields, and Richard Milne could not believe that she had spoken. Those fields, he remembered, while they became dreary and inanimate to him at memory of the many times he had returned to them in vain, these fields barrenly flourishing to the darkening oblivious forests, were her constant sight. He seized her still hand – he who had vowed never to touch her again until the availing outcome of his quest had appeared. He had seen it all many an evening before, and she – she had looked on few other vistas throughout her years. "What is it holds you, Ada?" he asked in a choking tone, as though she were dying before his eyes.

She did not stir, there was no motion of her body on the bench while her hand warmed in his, and she looked into the approaching night. With a long sigh, a smile, she turned, looked at her hands on the books, at him. At last, quietly:

"I don't know." She roused herself and smiled almost brightly at him. "Why are you here?" she asked, as though the question were as reasonable as his had been.

He made no answer, since they both knew that it was not necessary to mention why he had returned this time. Something made him understand that she had not changed, that surely in all this place of eroded dreams she was least changeable. And yet he knew as well that his spirits were rising as if in obedience to an old call, and he was about to press her with reasonings, expostulations she had heard often enough before, and which would pour from his lips in a flood. But she turned her eyes away and went on.

"I don't know, and I have admitted to you that there is no reason which would operate logically. But perhaps what holds me here is knowing that if I went my mother would die. She would starve, as completely – God knows it is precious little that I do or can do for her, and yet it is only my being here that keeps her soul alive. They have been estranged so long that they are really dead to each other, and yet if they were left alone together they would both, she, at least, would die the bodily death as well."

He smiled bitterly. "It is always of her you speak," he added, with a surprising acrimony, for his thwarted feeling was being transferred to annoyance in behalf of the representative of his own sex in this generation-long quarrel. "Doesn't your father feel? Do you think he doesn't know the bitter of loneliness and misprision as well as your mother?"

"Father, of course. I know that, and it is why things are as they are. Possibly if I could take sides, there could be some outcome, even to strife. But I see, I understand too well, so that there is no hope. I see the sadness of both, and how oblivion awaits it all . . . across a mist of pathos like dreaming."

"You're too sympathetic," said the man gruffly. He wanted to add that she had been thinking about it too much. "Surely something could be done. I tell you, it would be a tonic, a rough cold-blooded treatment. Why, they could have been laughed out of everything, or I'm mistaken. To go on in this way – it's absurd. . . ." But he spoke less from reason than desperation, with a maddeningly increasing sense of impotence in the smothering shroud of time and place, the over-powering creep of memories that die only to haunt implacably. "It's plain to me that your father has a good deal to complain of. Perhaps you don't know that there are many kinds of men with whom no – no such situation could exist."

"I hope so," she murmured, so that he could scarcely hear. The silence grew, big with all that they could not say, which neither could understand well enough to form into words, and yet which they felt between them like an impalpable tie.

"There are women who wouldn't let it exist," he continued, with a doggedness which ignored his paradox. But Ada did not smile.

"Well," sighed Richard Milne at last. "We don't seem to know that we have been apart for a long time."

They smiled, lost in a sense of this, of being together, and that each dearly-lost moment gave its measure of almost painful bliss. Looking at the clear profile of Ada Lethen, he felt his heart rise, as though it would break his body apart. The mazed night could have lasted forever, it might have been the beginning or end of eternity.

They exchanged little words, about his travels, how the village seemed to him, changes . . . almost as though shy. And a wave of tender memory came over Richard Milne at her questions, her concern. He saw those days mysterious and full of homely poetry, when he had been a boy in these fields – an evocation of weather, irrelevant transitory conditions, neighbours, above all the surveillance of these over the Lethen family, which had drawn to it his child's curiosity. The odd and vivid little girl of whom he was conscious sitting at one side and behind him in the schoolhouse; their awakening to each other which seemed without beginning; the silence between them, always the silence, and the forbidding looks which he read in the constraint of either of her parents he inadvertently met. The secret coming out at last from the mouth of gossip that wondered at his not always having known. All these made a medium through which translucently to see Ada Lethen – an image of sleet frozen upon maple buds.

"You do not love them," he continued slowly, half-unwilling to voice his thought. "But that does not cause you to change your attitude toward me. You're no kinder or more – reasonable. I dare say if you hated them you'd think that gave you the right, or the obligation to care for their needs." The cruelty of his suffering was speaking now.

"Hate? I can never hate them – it would be impossible." Yet she had answered so swiftly, with an involuntary look at him, that he felt he had probed her most secret dread. "Only pity. It is pity which – Pity will kill me!" she exclaimed with sudden wildness, as though the words themselves lent to her sense a foretaste of ultimate bitterness.

"I can't! I can't!"

She was sobbing words against his shoulder, while all his thoughts, the froth on the billow of his emotion flew scattered by this sudden contact. And he had come determined not to touch her hand, for the havoc it would be to him afterward. Now he held her, tightly, speaking incoherently.

"Precious Ada! This is going to kill you. Ada! Let us go away. You must! We can live a different life from this. We'll go —"

All the time her tears were changing something in his mind. The hot tears fell on his hands, and he began to try to comfort her. It was as though they were children again, and she had cried, as she did once, about something some of the other children said, and he had offered her his handkerchief. The years were broken up and their emotions returned upon him in a confused avalanche, while he held her, and at the same time he was in the present, his arms were holding her as they had longed to do.

"Let us go away!" he heard himself repeating in a tone of anguished pleading which was almost maudlin.

The night was flowing past them, through the trees, past them in cold vines of the veranda of the decayed house. And it seemed as though they were being left, stranded in an unimaginable waste beyond life, alone and not together, deserted even of hot and frenzied words, while the mystery of the earth and the skies became in imminence torturingly sweet.

FOUR

At this moment something made Richard Milne aware of a stirring in the room behind them. There was still light enough to show the figure of a woman, that woman who was sinister in his mind by very reason of her appalling and helpless misery. Her tall form bent over a vase of white narcissus. Other vases of the glowing white flower lent a distilled radiance to the dusk of the room. It seemed, though the window was down, that a sickly, heavy odour came spreading impalpable through the air. Richard seemed to be stupefied by it, and kept his watch in fascination; but the woman inside appeared unconscious of everything but the flowering bulbs. Her fingers caressed a blossom, and she passed to the other side of the room to look at a bulb just breaking into bud, with a slow, trembling shake of the head. She gazed a long time at this one, and long at one wilting with the accomplishment of its short life. She turned at last and passed into another room, opening and closing the door in silence peculiarly a summation of her white face.

He felt and heard a sigh at his cheek. "She can't have

heard us. . . ." The window was darkened by the Virginia Creeper.

"You speak as though nothing could be more terrible than her hearing us," he replied aloud. "As a matter of fact, it would probably be one of the best things which could happen if they overheard us – both of them – discussing them in the harshest and least sympathetic manner." His own surprised misgiving at the urgency of these words was only equalled by hers. She was struck silent in a way which made patent the effort with which she began speaking again.

"She has always loved the narcissi." Ada's cadence on that word "loved" was enough to show that her fear was well grounded, and that pity could drain her soul. Instead of seeing an unreal, almost delusive quality in the situation, as one fresh from the sane world, she appeared to conceive of no other reality beyond this abnormal state of affairs. She accepted wholeheartedly the fact of her mother and her mother's state, where one unobsessed would have implied, for all its gravity, a lightness of reservation.

"I remember," he assented heavily, with an accumulation of unspoken criticism in his tone. "But how does she endure them? A bulb or two is nice to have, if you like them, but such a number, with their enervating odour, must be intolerable to anyone else."

"But she likes them, worships them. She seems to think of nothing else from day to night. She looks at them, cares for them, she has some of them beside her when she sleeps, and first thing in the morning she comes downstairs to look at the others. I have known her to get up in the middle of the night to come downstairs to the sitting-room and look at them. Sometimes she will fall in a reverie over them, and I can scarcely call her away to a meal."

"Yes, she must be fairly fond of them," he assented grimly. "But how do you stand it? It must get on your nerves, doesn't it, day after day?" He was consciously trying to arouse her. "To say nothing of the smell. And she keeps the windows closed all the time?"

"Yes, nearly all the time. . . . Sometimes I plead with her, but I think it does no good, it does harm. She becomes secretive, and starts when I come into the room and she is with them."

Richard was almost ready to feign such brutality as casual curiosity would dictate. "It's pathological," he muttered. "Should be looked into."

"They've always been so much to her, a refuge for her yearning, since I seem inanimate and averse. And – more now – And then –" He could see that she was struggling with the obviousness of some feeling which was obscurely trying to make her refer to her father.

Richard Milne smiled bitterly at the conception of her as inanimate and averse, but he said:

"And your father still means more to her than she admits or knows, though she would cut her heart out to be rid of him –" There was a weary flippancy almost of cynicism in his utterance, as of one arming himself with brusqueness against too many torturing perplexities. Again there was an upward inflection here suddenly warily deceitful, though he would not openly question her; for while he knew the outward circumstances of this quandary, never yet had he known Ada Lethen to talk about it in the way he wished, as though she expected or even hoped that he could understand.

"That is to be expected," she answered, with a tinge of coldness, "seeing the source of it all. Had it been any ordinary quarrel which tempted them into declaring in the frenzied tones I remember, that they would never speak to each other again – the bitterness might have, it must have, lapsed, passed away in the lukewarm tolerance with which most people must regard each other."

It came to him that she was a stranger to the warmth and coolness of ordinary domestic relations and family inter-course. An uncanny thrill was imparted with her words, as if they had embodied an exercise of intuition on the part of an immigrant from another planet, but hardly inured to the life of this; and he could have wept to think of that little girl.

"You – you were present at the quarrel, the original one?" He dared not ask, and yet he must.

Yes, she told him. The child had sat at the head of the stairs, shivering in her nightgown, and she heard it all. The raised voices went on for hours, and, as in the height of a storm, it always seemed that violence could reach no further pitch and these emotions would come to outrageous ends. "I'll never forget how I shivered, and my heart went when I thought they meant to kill one another. But at last I fell asleep there." She went on with added constraint in her tone, "And there I was in the morning." They had passed her, the woman to her room, the father to get his coat in the hall. Neither had touched the child, though they had passed so near as almost to step over its insensible form.

His arm went out to her again. "Poor little thing! I'm afraid I can never understand all that your childhood was; only pity. But what you say does not tend to make me pity – these people. Quite the contrary."

In an instant, while he sat there unmoving, unchanged in aspect, a flame of rage had wrapped him as a tree may be robed in fire, leaving him for the moment gripped helpless and listening only half-consciously to her words.

"You shouldn't pity me," she murmured, and continued, "it must have been that, perhaps, rather than my rational intelligence, which taught me to be cold to both of them. Perhaps if any love for either of them had been left afterward my heart should have been broken. As it is –" She laughed bitterly.

"You know that as it is I am heartless." Yet this speech and the eyes with which she looked at him as she said it made Richard Milne wonder and hope. Clearly there had been a change, and she must have learned in his absence to admit to herself whether or not she loved him. The thought was enough: with mounting surety he felt she did love him, that this was the time appointed – that surely he and Ada Lethen would not let go the chance of happiness without a struggle. If only it were just a matter of duty. But it was not. For so much of her life she had been bound to this place and to these slowly petrifying people that she could not imagine herself apart from them.

Perhaps the knot of the whole difficulty lay there. Desperately as she might yearn, he felt that she could not conceive happiness. Perhaps nothing but the death of one of those parents would bring her awake – alone – drive her to living.

"Your heart was too tender for such storms. It makes me wild to think of it – to think of your sitting there, hearing –" The vividness of the picture he saw caused him to wince away from its unbelievable pathos, its meagre sharpness, like the outline of a remote folk-story, suddenly quickened to life by the lips of one of its participants.

"I think I could repeat every word," she said quietly. "They – each thought the other unfaithful. They proved that each was certain, no matter how much the other denied it, and that they would be obliged by every human consideration to hate each other to the end of life. And they have never spoken to each other since."

"Never?" He mused with what seemed an idle particularity. His mind had accepted the fact long since, so that it did not occur to him to brand this inveterate silence as insane and foreign to humanity. Everyone in his boyhood world had accepted it.

Night had set in, wild as autumn; out in the open wind tore the darkness, the trees sighed loud, and colour was given to strain. Among the sheltered recesses of the lawn, about the thick evergreen trees, the hedge, and the veranda, the occasionally flawed quietude allowed the mind, lulled and affrighted anew, to return again and again to the turbulence without. A cricket or crickets took up their cry, silenced, and returned. What portion could there be, what human portion, but a strife of futility, meaningless turmoil? To watch it was to be lulled, only to hear were peace; and he looked at her face, hoping to hear her voice go on, sweetening the acrid past. But she said nothing, the moment was gone; and on the flood of many remembered longings and resolves surged back his single intent.

"Ada!" he burst out. "This is absurd. For anyone who could do that, much as I might ultimately pity them, it's impossible to find excuse or condolence. To pamper them emotionally all this time is ridiculous. As your parents they will receive my respect; not otherwise, I assure you. You know as well as I that unless some definite course is undertaken nothing can be hoped."

"A course! What course?" she half moaned.

"But," he adjured her, "if you let things take their own way there is bound to be a great deal of trouble and bitterness. You will find that you have acquired nothing for the furnishing of your life but sorrow and the memories of sorrow. You are even farther removed than my own ideals are from the

33

dogma of to-day. That arrivism, opportunism, at best only cloaks the thirst for getting which is rendering barren the lives we see everywhere. Materialism. Yet in a degree we've got to recognize that it is based on the reality which is foundation to material things. People get it reversed and think that material things are the only basis of reality. But it is our destiny: we are bound to conquer. We must subdue things; we've got to take from life even the emotions, the experience, and fulfilment we need. If we shirk that we are doing a wrong as great as that of starving in the midst of nature's abundance." Words had betrayed him again. He did not know whether she were listening.

"There's no use talking, sacrifice is all right. It is part of the acceptance of life. Calmness and freedom from inordinate grasping is good. But the fact which you and I have to face right now is that happiness is not offered for ever in this world, it does not go begging; and we have a right to all of it we can make, a duty to ourselves which is imperative and primary, and only the fruition of which enables us to do a duty to others."

She said nothing. He knew that she agreed with him, and that her agreement would make no difference. She was not to be aroused by the acrimony of the first part of his harangue, nor by the reasons of his special plea. Though he spoke with a cool voice, emphatic intonations, and at times almost judicial deliberation, he had become warmed so that her inert silence met him like a chill barrier. He felt that he had talked the "sales-talk" of a "go-getter" of his city, city like an enthusiastic nightmare of another planet now.

What is there in her face, he asked himself with a sudden frenzied access, what is there in her soul, that has made me return, time after time – made my nights a memory and my days a double vision? Love? It was to laugh at the simplicity of the tiny word. Who had told that love was torture of the being, that love would blast life from him in a flutter of trivialities as oak-leaves are loosed upon the wind after the first frost? Who had told him that love would eat beneath his comfort in accomplishment until he knew himself in his wanderings a lost soul? Beneath everything, his most cherished activities, lay a weary impatience with them and a sense of their irrelevance in the lack of a determining motive to channel their force.

She turned to him, and it was as though she had descried a vision of beatification in the darkness; she took his hand as though she would warm it in her cold hand. But the light in her face slowly died as her low voice, with pauses, unwonted uncertainties here and there, went on. Again, as though tranced, he had nothing but to listen, given up not to her reasonings, but to her, the spirit beneath, which embraced not only them and her conduct, but the very qualities which made her to him what she was. And it was her hand which was warmed, though a gesture lifted both to her breast.

"Richard, I know. That is what makes it so hard, that I do understand. Oh, don't think I don't want happiness, that I am harsh. But I have found the hardest thing to do. . . . I see Father going about the farm as though he were lost; and his hair is white. . . . Like his horses, he is old; like them, he is patient, even in waiting for the end. What should I be doing to leave him? There is some other way. My mother seems daily to give her frail life to the white narcissi; and, while she is not old, she makes me fear the more. You can see how it is with me, and how I must not listen to – the outer world, even to – even as I have. . . ." Her voice broke as if from a weight of longing which would return in days after.

Richard Milne's impelling desperation would no longer be kept within bounds. He seemed to find her pleas unanswerable as she had his. He rose from the seat. His voice quivered. A fear that they were cutting themselves off from each other as they had done before did not suffice to temper his embittered discomfiture, which he scarcely cloaked in polite circumstantiality.

"It is late and I must not keep you, Ada. We must talk again," he added with a perverse effort at balance. He was facing the window giving on the dark room; across it he saw the crack of light under the door, which showed that life went on in the rear portions of the house. "I hope my intrusion hasn't kept your mother too long from her bulbs." To this irrepressible malice in jejune and childish politeness Ada made a vague gesture and rose as he went on: "I am going to have to talk with your parents. They, too, may not be able to understand reason and common logic, but at least they shall listen. It is late now, and I shall not disturb them."

She put out her hand. "I'm sorry, Richard." She said it so simply and with such significance that his anger melted, and he half felt that he was defeated once more. Then his stubborn pugnacity whelmed the feeling. He grasped her extended hand.

"Give them my regards, please, and tell them that. We'll see."

Smiling a little at his grimness, the tall woman murmured:

"I'm sure they'll be glad to see you again. They have so few visitors, and they remember you, of course. Father was asking why you hadn't seen him the last time you were here."

"I look at the whole thing differently now," he declared

again. "I must see them both regardless of any kind interest they may have in me."

Ada Lethen became grave. "Richard, you mustn't look at it in that way. There's nothing to get angry about, nothing to be done." She looked at him with steadfast, upraised eyes.

"That remains to be seen, and will be seen. Good night, Ada."

Smiling a little, she stood on the veranda and watched him quickly swallowed in the gloom of the night, his footsteps muffled by the grass and pine needles, by the wind roaring above him, wrapping him with huge tatters in the road.

He was gone.

FIVE

He did not seem to have slept at all before strange noises, shoutings, silences, came and went in what he knew was dreaming. Strangely, actual seconds only made a dream of the reality from which, tossing, he had tried through the night to find surcease. They merged with dozing unbelief in his return – so ineffectual – and his presence in a place alienated which should have welcomed him. . . . Richard Milne rose, bumping his head upon the gable ceiling, and stepped to the open window.

Dawn had come, lifting sharp colour from the fields. In a haze of level yellow sunshine on the dusty lane below, Carson Hymerson and his son manoeuvred and spoke, the voices ringing back from the shady, cliff-like barns at the far side of the yard. The skeleton of a hayrake stood between them, and they were fitting teeth into a long horizontal bar. Richard Milne had an impulse to laugh at the oblivious and loud-voiced preoccupation. Carson bent, showing patches on the back of faded clothes, clawed the air at one side of him without turning his head, and spoke with injured tones of imperial dudgeon.

"There! You've let loose and they're slipped out again. Give me that piece of wire! . . . Show 'em!"

Arvin, a tall, bowed young man with prominent, aquiline features, went to the wire fence of the lane and lifted from it the piece which providentially hung there. His father viciously twisted the wire about the wooden bar and the rod on which the teeth were strung. It was evident that it would be impossible to insert the teeth between them.

"Now! What you gawpin' at me for? You've let the others loose, and now they've jumped out of the holes. If ever I see –"

Arvin, who had been contemplating his father's mistake, said nothing, but hastily jumped to the other end of the bar and held it against the teeth. His father continued to whine, until he said abruptly:

"Well! You told me to get the wire, and now see what you've done."

"You're too smart!" shouted his father without rancour. "It's all your fault. You just think we shouldn't be doing it ourselves, that's all, and you won't help."

The son digested this a moment, seeming about to speak, and then to think better of it.

"It's all right for you to talk," went on the older man, turning the teeth of the rake on the steel rod delicately until they hung loosely in a perfect row. "Yes, eh, send it to the blacksmith; don't do anything yourself for fear of getting your hands dirty. No, I'm not farming that way just yet. . . . I don't say but what if I was gone, stowed away safe enough under ground, there'll be enough of that goes on, but not just to-day, thank you, too rich for my blood. That ain't how the old pioneers got along. If your grandfather could see the slouchy way you do things, he'd turn over in his grave. Reach me that chisel. . . ."

"Yeh, I bet he'd –"

"Don't you leave go!" yelled Hymerson. "People are getting more shiftless all the time. For a certainty."

Richard Milne stared half-awake from his window, and the argumentative, swift whine, with outbursts of shouting, the quiet, occasional remonstrance of the younger man ascended to him as though he were watching a play; until with a start he straightened and returned to bed. They even pursued him there. So he was back amid the oblivion of the farmer's cares! It was a rousing reality. The possibility of sleep was gone for that night, and, seeing that it was nearly six o'clock according to the thin watch under his pillow, he dressed. In the kitchen he greeted Mrs. Hymerson, who was holding a slice of bread on a fork over the lidless hole of the wood stove.

"I've been going to get me a regular toaster," she remarked offhandedly, "but I haven't got around to it yet." Richard wondered what formalities connected with the man of the house would be necessary before this could be accomplished. Meanwhile it seemed likely that smoke would contribute as much as heat to the texture of the toast. "I didn't put your hat in the front hall," she added, as instinctively the young man reached to the nail behind the door. "Doesn't seem right to treat you like ordinary company so much –"

Outside the shade was chill and the air quiet, as though the trees had forgotten the struggle with the wind of the night before. The dust of the lane appeared to have been swept by it, smoothed from so much as a leaf upon the surface. The spirit of those gusty hours had belatedly entered Carson Hymerson.

"If he does stay it'll be all right for us. He won't know anything about it and people won't –"

The farmer was still ejaculating and gesturing, unaware of his guest's approach. Arvin tried to warn him of it by smiling and leaving the rake with outstretched hand to greet his early friend. "Here! What's the idea –" Then the other saw too.

Arvin Hymerson was perhaps an inch taller than Richard Milne when he straightened, and his rather bashful smile was not belied by the freshet of reminiscent inquiry with which such meetings are accompanied. Still the interest was there, real, and Richard Milne found himself feeling that he had been away perhaps two weeks. For the first time he fully realized his return. When the weather had been canvassed Arvin said:

"We're fixing up the old side-delivery rake. Kind of late getting around to it, but we thought we'd better do it ourselves instead of sending it to the blacksmith."

The older man looked up from the teeth of the rake and grinned mockingly.

"Arvin here's been buying a cow. I was just telling him he'd ought to have been making a regular study of the market before he went out. Then he'd been sure not to get beat."

Richard smiled. "Oh, I should think that Arvin must know a good deal about cattle, Mr. Hymerson. I don't think I'd care to have a trade with him myself." He was not accusing Arvin of dishonesty. He found himself sympathetically taking on the attitude and locutions of a former time.

"Not 'less you wanted to get beat, eh?" The man was somewhat mollified. "Well, go and look at his cow. Just go and look at it, and see what you think of the bargain. I'll tell you how much he gave afterwards." A challenging malice spoke here, as though his son were not present.

The latter, Richard Milne reflected after looking at the cow, a goodly and not noteworthy Shorthorn, deserved consideration for his patience; for his industry also, since the floors of the cow stable were as spotless as its whitewashed cement walls. As though conscious of his friend's attitude, Arvin remarked:

"Litter-carriers. Farming's not so bad as it used to be. Things are getting a little handier."

They stood talking a few minutes at the doorway of the stable, which framed a green and grey landscape, and then went to breakfast. Richard Milne found himself in good spirits and inclined to play the part of the well-entertained guest. This would not hurt his cause with Mrs. Hymerson, he knew. He had decided not to go back to the city, and to let it rest with her whether he was to stay, "spend his vacation," in that house. From Carson Hymerson, he divined, anything, or nothing, might be expected.

The farmer had changed considerably with the years, from the young man's memory of him – a surreptitiously waggish, brisk fellow taking chop to mill, striding about the muddy streets in a yellow raincoat and rubber boots, laughing and joking with other farmers on the steps of the store. This present swiftness of speech, innuendo, and attitude of not being taken in by anybody, was perhaps the result of forces in the man which the years could not but have brought out. Richard Milne had never ceased to admire the peripety of life, its myriad fugacious shadings like lake tints which become more intricate to the sight with care in scrutinizing them.

As they came out of the house after breakfast a team of horses emerged from alders around the bend of the road, with a two-wheeled implement surmounted by a barrel. On this a boy sat as though precariously, for it was perched horizontally, and looked ready to roll off. Two low, chair-like seats under and behind the barrel almost dragged the ground between the wheels.

"Tobacco-planter," Arvin told him.

"Yes, that's a tobacco-planter!" added Hymerson, as though it were a grim joke.

"Dad don't like the tobacco. Won't grow it. I keep telling him we're going to lose out, with tobacco the price it is. . . ."

"I guess, eh! I wouldn't have the dirty stuff on my place, let alone smoke it, put the dirty stuff in my mouth. Agh! They can have it, them fellows." He went, with swinging steps and one arm held out, toward the pig-pen, a swill-pail brushing his bulky, stiffened overalls at every step. Arvin grinned, looking from him to Richard Milne.

He, too, went to the stable, and hitched a team to the rake. When he had gone creaking down the lane Richard followed the older man about while he did the chores, tended to the needs of the stock, and prepared another meal for them. Then they walked over the rolling, wooded farm together. Carson said, as they crossed a hollow along a hap-hazard rail fence:

"That's how he looks after things, that old man. Won't even keep up the line fence between neighbours. I've had about enough of it, never keeping the fences fixed, letting the cattle run – even hogs."

Pausing to light a cigar, Milne asked thoughtfully, "Why don't you make some settlement, say, have it that – if this is Lethen's end of the line – that the fence should be fixed by him, or, if not, that you will do so at his expense? I should think that some arrangement could be made." He was tired of the man's complaints, and still more of his rancorous air of compunction.

"Oh, that wouldn't hardly do. Might get to be bad friends with him, that way." Carson glanced at him in alarm and joggled the two forks on his shoulder.

"I don't see the point," murmured Richard. He knew that Hymerson would talk about his injuries to any listener, and generally comport himself as though in fact a breach existed between the neighbours. At the hayfield which Arvin was raking Carson began to bunch a windrow, but Richard did not accept the hint of the extra fork – let him stand it in the ground and went away.

He walked across the fields and woods in the general direction of the village. It was a day of the perfected tranquillity which only June can match, and which even in June one feels unmatchable. The clouds in their quietude only gave surcease from warmth and brilliance to the surfeited vegetation and trees, only varied that intense blue which had not yet lost its softness of spring, and which, it seemed, could never take on the greenish bitterness of first snow, the darkness of autumn storm.

The young man wandered for a time with the sense of well-being and careless optimism tempering more individual feeling, even curious recognition of old landmarks. And the fields were remarkably little changed. Toward the river the banks, the dredged ditches leading into it, the hedges of underbrush, preserved the old contours, and new fencing was in evidence more usually in the fields nearer the fronts of the farms and along the road. The lanes were the same as those down which he had wandered in earliest times to the bush for wild-flowers in spring and nuts in autumn. Richard Milne sat curiously aimless on a weathered, grey rail fence, looking at a rusty disc harrow with a homemade log tongue, to which bark still adhered. A huge, battered, old leather shoe had been nailed to the tongue for a tool-box.

He was impressed anew with the true reasonableness of farm practice. There was that about it which might appear elsewhere inertia and shiftlessness. If an appliance served its appointed purpose it was allowed to do so. There was no fever for the spick and span, and even glittering new-painted machinery soon took on protective colouring and comfortable, crude patchings. This was part of the nature of farming, and when it was overruled it was at the sacrifice of practical utility. He recalled visiting the farm of two graduates of an agricultural college, and how his expectations of a stricter formalization had been disappointed. Luckily farming did not lend itself to the simplifications of hospital wards, scientific laboratories, prisons. His experience with other departments of the modernized world led him to thank God for it.

At the end of a field of oats, so sparse and short that he skirted the patch as though in fear of injuring it, he came on a long, grey, fine-clodded field divided into narrow rows formed by the packed pattern of broad wheels. They belonged to a tobacco-planter, he guessed, because the tiny plants were in evidence, withered almost to nothing. And there was a man not far from the other end of the field, stooping over a row. Picking his way, Richard Milne advanced toward the figure. It strode to meet him, carrying a basket and a pail a few steps, then stooping, piercing a hole in the dry earth with a blunt stick, pouring water into the hole from the pail, and taking a plant from the basket, planted it. By the time he could follow this procedure he could see the man distinctly, his gaunt angular movements of stooping, planting, his swift strides forward, while the eyes were busy with the ground before him, seeking unplanted spaces and withered plants which must be replaced. In the gait and these gestures there was something familiar, and he lingered, trying to remember before he should have passed. He was on the old home place, on Bill Burnstile's farm. That was it!

But Bill was not going to let him pass. Lit by the sun under a drooping straw hat as tanned as itself, his face was leanly smiling.

"Well, here's the Stranger!" he exclaimed, stretching forth his hand. "My boys told me you were here yesterday. I couldn't hardly believe it."

Their hands held. "Fine family, Bill. I was certainly surprised too. When did you come back from the West?"

"Oh, we came back about a year ago. Well, a year last winter. Time certainly flies. You're looking well, though I can't say I'd have known you in a crowd. Pretty pale," he chuckled, "like a city fellow. Oh, well, the sun out here, the open air, you'll soon get brightened up." He looked at Richard Milne with jovial compunction, as though he were semi-invalid. That was the way, Richard knew, in which he regarded all city men, categorically.

"Yes. Healthful weather just now. How are your crops, Bill? Clover seems to have a pretty good stand around here. What happened to everybody's oats?"

Bill Burnstile's lantern jaws opened in a vast "Haw, haw!" and he bent back. "You certainly ain't forgot all about farming, I can tell you that much."

Richard Milne could not imagine anyone else of the locality making such distinctions. Of course, impervious stolidity might have its compensations. . . . In rural people it was often a part of instinctive caution.

It had been impossible, Bill was explaining, to put in the oats at the proper time. The ground was too wet, and even so lots of men had had to dub them in, any way to get them in, hopeless of good weather, and determined to have a few for their horses at least. Altogether it had not been a very good season. Now there was this drought. The bad weather was not ended yet, or he was mistaken. Still, there couldn't be a failure in everything – like in the West, where grain constituted the main asset. There a crop failure meant something.

"It was our West, of course," mused Richard. "When a Canadian 'goes West,' it usually means the Canadian West."

"Yes. . . . Have you been out yet?" The loose-jointed fellow seemed to take root in the ground, as though to stay there indefinitely talking.

"No. I'm sorry to say it, but I've never been there yet, not explored much of the world at all."

"Oh, I understood you had become a regular Yankee by this time. I was wondering whether we'd ever have you back with us at all or not. That's how it turns out, you know, when they get away once."

"On the contrary, this place has scarcely been out of my mind. Naturally, when one's been raised. . . . Do you find it changed at all since your return?"

"Well, no, can't say I do. Of course, they grow more tobacco than they ever did. That began in the War, of course. Then there were a couple of years there they had to give away what they had. Over-production, I guess, or some warfare between the companies. That was just about the time I got back, and it looked kind of silly to me. But some way I got around to thinking it may be all right to put a few acres in. I see the other fellows doing it, anyway. Of course, I got enough of putting all my eggs in the one basket out West. When there's rust, frost, or anything, hail, you just naturally lose your year's work."

The lank, brown, musing face was wrinkled. Richard saw a spear or two of white in his yellow temples. The man was changed and unchanged. The West, its gambling hazards, even a roving life had seemed more fitting to him than his present situation. He had been the dare-devil hail-fellow to innumerable scrapes in his youth in this circumscribed place. But then, he had met a woman, acquired a wife, the Waterloo of that character.

It was a fate, Richard Milne thought he saw, which had completely humanized the harum-scarum; or, if not completely, so well that he was now to be counted upon for half-conscious, humorous understanding: in effect, since a descent to the practical was inevitable, for support. Having seen the world and touched the commonplace of romance, he would rightly estimate the commonplace, and see its quartz-glitter in the dust of his hands.

No, he would not be suspecting these things in himself, and that would make half his value in a self-conscious world such as Richard Milne had come to know. A true man, which is something different from a nice fellow, his tough, lean body, his brown, lean face told something about him; he was as old now as he had looked ten years ago, as he would be in ten years' time. For his hearer the remarkable thing, so frequently invoked in print, was that here was a gentleman who had never read a book.

Meanwhile he, too, was stirred by the meeting, while the talk went on of crops. Only when such matters had been dealt with very thoroughly was it that Richard, about to leave, spoke again of the family.

"Yes, you've got to see the wife and our boys and girls while you're here. We're a regular tribe now. When I look at you, only a couple of years, ain't it, younger, it seems hard to believe."

"Well, we've both been away a long time. Time enough to have acquired a wife, you know." His tone was somewhat grim, though he tried to veil it with a smile.

"Well," declared the other in his turn, "my luck changed just as soon as we got married. And now, with a family, I've got to keep pegging away, so it doesn't seem to have a chance to change." He laughed.

"That's good. Why, here they come now!"

A sound echoing from the trees at the end of the field made them turn. A boy and a girl were running toward them, halfway across, while two little boys were climbing the fence. As they ran barefoot over the soft, even, warm ground, with cries back and forward to each other, light-hearted, breathless, light-footed, Richard Milne stood transfixed for a second, permeated with a sense of his own childhood. Intently looking at the stranger, and their father, expecting who knew what cryptic spoken index of the mysterious world of which they guessed only that it was wonderful, they came forward.

"Well, you're puffing, Bill." The older Bill put his hand on the boy's bristling yellow head, half shoving playfully. "This is Alice," he added of the girl, whom Richard had seen on the road the day before. "This gentleman used to live here when he was as little as you."

"This farm, this very farm?" Bill wanted to know.

"Right here," the man assented, smiling. "But I used to be everywhere, when I could get away."

"A great rover you used to be, Dick. Remember when we used to go for hickory nuts to old Broadus's place? Nobody else's was as good, because he didn't want us."

."Now, here come Johnnie and Tom," laughed Alice. "They couldn't stay away."

The two raced up in silence, even more nearly breathless than the others. "He's going to let me plant 'em," gasped a seven-year-old chubby, dark boy, not stopping to pant, but seizing the basket in his father's hand. He looked up, his long, silky lashes glistening, his dark skin shining. He was like a sleek baby animal, and somehow different from the others. They eyed his manoeuvre with misgiving, and knew better than to try to take the basket from him. The third boy, who had run with him, was evidently the oldest, thin, tall, stooped, with open mouth and light eyes.

"Now we've lots of help," mused Bill Burnstile. "I'm kind of juberous about letting you go at it; but maybe, if your sister looked after you, you could do a good job. Suppose Bill carries the basket, and Tom takes the plant out of it, while Johnnie here punches the hole with the stick. Alice can walk along behind and see that you keep straight in line with the row. And don't waste the plants, and don't miss any out. Give Bill the basket now, Johnnie." The dark eyes were hurt, but Johnnie took his assigned part.

"This drought makes it bad," Burnstile explained, once more turning to his visitor. "I kept working the ground up to keep the moisture in, and waiting for a rain. Got her in finally, day before yesterday, but no rain yet to help much."

"It makes a lot of work, when you've got to go over the whole field this way and transplant." Richard laughed, looking at the group of children hurrying down the row, stopping in a bunch, then running on. "Seems funny to see these infants planting tobacco. One thinks of nobody but men having been near that. Carson Hymerson was telling me this morning he doesn't approve of growing it."

"Carson's funny. Of course, it's hard on the land. But that isn't why he doesn't grow it."

"A more personal objection?" Richard raised his eyebrows.

"Seems like it. Arvin, he's grown to be quite a sensible fellow, though. And that's a wonder. He's sure working under disadvantages. Why, the boy can't open his mouth, can't say it's a fine day, but what the old man wants to argue. He'll argue black's white just to make out the boy's a liar. Doesn't matter to Carson that he's got to seem one himself. Perhaps he wants to provoke the boy to calling him one. What he does want I don't know, nor I guess he don't neither. It's a wonder Arvin doesn't give him such a back-hander! With me he wouldn't live long, or I wouldn't. Oh, he's a tartar."

"I seemed to see some change in the man. Something's wrong. Something seems to be troubling him."

"Well," said Bill Burnstile consideringly, "I've been among gangs of men, and I know just about how long he'd keep a whole skin if he acted that way. . . ."

"He seems," Milne insisted on the word, "to have worries about the line fence between himself and Lethen. He was telling me a good deal about that."

"He would. You'll find out what an awful man poor old man Lethen is. Haw, haw! Carson, he hasn't bothered me much yet, and I suppose he's got to size me up. I don't think he will, either."

"Does Mr. Lethen farm all of his own land himself?" Richard cared little that he was exaggerating the casual tone of his query.

"No; this tobacco's been a good thing for him. He fits up a few acres, and lets it on shares, and makes a little money that way. The rest of the farm he pastures, and grows some stuff on. Of course, he can't keep a hired man," said Bill Burnstile, looking him in the eyes. "Never has for years and years, they tell me. You'd know all about that, of course, as well as me. A fellow's got to feel sorry for him."

"It seems that nothing has changed. . . ." Richard's voice was tinged by a fleeting memory of those very words between himself and Ada Lethen.

"Naw." The gaunt man spat. "Of course, there's something there you and me can't make out. I guess old lady Lethen is all right, from what I've always gathered. It just seems funny these days. I've heard my father talk about people who never spoke to each other, but I never come across but those two. . . . Makes it hard for the girl. Now she's smart, right sensible. If they would let her alone she'd fix things up, run the farm – there must be a mortgage – in no time, just like nothing; good head on her. But them – why they don't seem livin'."

"Strange existence," mused the young man, wondering at the interest generated, and impelling the man's words.

"You understand me, they don't seem alive," continued Bill argumentatively. "Now when I'd go over there to borrow a tool or something, and get to the door, the old lady would be so polite, just as nice as pie, ask about the family, tell me where she thought I might find the old man, and all that. But if he wasn't home, no use leaving any message with her. Might as well save your breath. She'd never tell him anything if it was going to save you from the grave. Makes it unhandy that way for the neighbours."

Richard Milne roused himself from the reverie which he knew might divert the interest of his companion, and, without replying to the reference to Ada Lethen, took leave, after promising to visit the family some day soon.

SIX

Somehow the day had become overcast for him. It was as though a shadowy thought of happiness had been driven from his mind by some intervening emergency, and now he could not even recall in what this mood consisted. Probably it was no more than morning hope and healthy spirits. And those were as likely to be illusion as the anonymous doubt which was now filling his mind. At least he could not blame Bill Burnstile. He should have been – he was, he told himself – gratified by the encounter with his old friend of his boyhood, now a man, honest, simple, rough, real, true to himself, and open-eyed to what reality came his way.

It was what the man had told of the Lethens which bothered him. Somehow he must have thought that he possessed the secret in his own right, and that, possessing it, he might be able alone to unfathom the riddle. Behold now, though, others had watched, baffled, even dispirited as himself by the sight. Bill Burnstile had talked as though absorbed by the subject, though without ulterior intent; and Carson Hymerson spoke with bitterness. Richard could not help wondering whether all the neighbours were so deeply concerned, whether an atmosphere had not been caused to rise about these people which would forever forbid his imposing reality or recognition upon them. In what reality did they believe? What could he have believed in Ada Lethen's place?

He was sitting on an old wooden gate at the head of a green lane which sloped down into a farm, with no buildings in sight, and he jumped off to continue his walk when he saw the girl before him. He paused. It was Ada Lethen who came up to him. The stateliness which he had known in the dusk of last night was modified by a languor which must have been weariness, for he saw that she was really thin. Her smile quite transfigured her dark, pale face; her eyes remembered themselves in a glint of happiness, looking at him steadfastly.

"You're going the wrong way," he told her with an assumption of country jocosity. It seemed that for surprise of joy he could have leaped the high gate before her.

"I am? I hadn't any particular place in view –"

"Just out for a walk?" he interrupted urgently. "Then you may as well come with me."

She looked back over her shoulder at the forest into which the lane ran. "But I just did come out of that bush. I rather expected," she drawled softly, "that there might be some wild flowers there. Perhaps I'm too late. But then I didn't happen to think of them before. . . ."

"Never too late! Orange lilies, jack-in-the-pulpits, we'll find some! Come. I must explore the whole country while I'm here!"

They walked along the grass of the wide, rail-fenced lane, down and up the slopes of which twined branching cow-paths, worn in other years by droves of belling, tranquil animals. The morning was passing in a mellow green quiet, which seemed to Richard Milne loud with another clamour than that of the city: his awakened hopes, a tumult of memories and desire. Looking at her beside him, he heaved a great breath and said:

"I can hardly believe it, but here I am. Here are you, what's more. Here are we!" he sang suddenly in the echoes of the trees. "Whatever foundling gods take the place of Pan, we are here!"

She smiled slightly at his enthusiasm of a boy; her generous lips seemed trembling to a smile as they walked. "I'm inclined not to come out very often. I think to-day is the first since winter that I have left the farm like this. In winter, spring, autumn, it's good to come and see that there is growth, change, and death, nothing of which is bitter or gay, simply because it does return again. It does return again. . . . Yet in that way, too, it is very precious. But you don't wish me to be serious," she laughed.

He was silent, not knowing how to convey his risen spirits, and not daring to try for fear of jarring on her mood. She had kept inviolate for a few far-parted days of the year this desire to commune with nature, and had avoided the chafing with which day-by-day intercourse would have blunted her love. And this to her was everything, everything tangible of beauty beyond the poignant and trivial dullness of her days. After all, she scarcely had realized, save as a rumour, that there was another world beyond these fields. Had she not known the world of poetry, ideas, she perhaps would not have been conscious of loving them, nor ever have known the fear of love, that fear that she could grow to hate them, though her bitterness would be the mere working of monotony. Then she would wish that, like the clod-like people about her, she had never learned to love them. She looked about her with quiet eyes, not asking of the forest that it be to them rest from vain study, but that it be its strange self as it had been to her child-hood memories, when in earlier spring she never forgot to come out for wild flowers, and sometimes little Dick Milne went beside her, and they raced each other to clustered violets or more common wet-rooted mayflowers, shy lady-slippers.

They paused as they had done in those times, and looked up the long trunks of rough trees, to the feathery, cloudy upper branches, and there, as in an old afternoon, circled a crane, its long, thin legs and neck stuck straight out against the sky: soared and soared in the opening above the feathery boughs, huge, until they thought they were staring up phantom trees, pillars of a dream, immeasurably high.

"Oh, it makes me dizzy!" The girl lowered her head.

"We must have looked up quite a while," the man mut-tered. "Ada, do you remember the time we saw a crane when we were children? We stared and stared just the same, and you were dizzy that time too. Seems impossible to believe that bird's not going to do something interesting. Does he see our faces in the rift of treetops, and wonder what those strange, wavering bulbs are going to do, whether they are a menace or . . . The bush is drier now than it was in those days. I remem-ber it was all pools under the trees, brown with dead leaves. I thought you were going to fall into one when you became dizzy looking up."

"It's later now . . . later in the year."

They walked forward. "And the land all about is drained now. How vast the bush seemed, and echoey then. Now we know how few acres it is, and how small a mystery."

They spoke of a girlhood and boyhood it seemed impos-sible to know would never return. It seemed that they had been nearer together then than now or at any time during the long siege of her. He remembered the first day Ada had gone to school at the little frame schoolhouse at the cross-roads, and how he and she had walked home on opposite sides of the road, along the ditch banks without a word. Soon they became friends and compared the lunches which they carried to school in tin pails, and shared them at noon. The teasing of the older children stopped this, and they did not pay much attention to each other during the day at school. But they always walked home together, until a new family moved to a neighbouring farm and provided Ada with the company of other girls. Later they walked together when the privilege of carrying her books had come to mean much to Richard.

Through these years he had been scarcely aware of her parents save as a rumour in the mouths of other children. Grown people seemed to keep silence about them. They must have been utterly indifferent to anything the little girl did away from their sight. She never spoke of them, and you could not think of her with them. She seemed perfect alone, needing no one. She was neatly dressed at school, on occasion came to Sunday school with neighbour girls, and looked a distinct and exotic creature among them. Scarcely ever in his memory had he seen Mrs. Lethen. Once she had been driving past in a buggy with Ada, and picked him up. He had never forgotten the consciousness of her presence under the narrow buggy-top as they drove down the muddy road.

Mr. Lethen was seen more, at threshing tables, in neighbours' houses, at meetings of the municipal council, of the school ratepayers, and so forth. He was not disposed to take a keen interest in his duties as a citizen, but his neighbours, knowing him a man of intelligence and some education, from time to time pressed him into certain offices. He was known to have queer ideas, and by some this was laid to his being educated, and by others to his year-long misunderstanding with his wife; while others took it as one of the reasons the two had not been able to get on together. More of the women, however, sympathized with him than the men. Farming indifferently, he pursued a casual course among his neighbours, as though there was nothing to be remarked about him, and it was quite ordinary to live a life with neither an impelling motive nor the warmth of family ties.

He never appeared in public with Mrs. Lethen, and when it was necessary to have people in the house she was not present. On her side, she avoided association with other women, often did not answer knocks at the door, and one who came of an afternoon to call was likely to go away puzzled. It was something to be marvelled at that their life could continue in the community and the family take its part therein as an efficient unit, while Mrs. Lethen remained apart, indifferent, or malign, present-in-absence.

Her hold on her daughter became more apparent as the girl grew up, and a second estrangement, Richard Milne recalled, had come between him and Ada Lethen. She seemed to grow away from him. Music had been her passion, and she had lent herself to it wholly. Her parents, indulgent or indifferent, had allowed her unchecked progress with elementary teachers, local girls returned from the Toronto conservatory, who insisted that Ada must "go on" with her "wonderful touch." Who knew what triumph of musical splendour might yet be released? Music – it was the impelling passion of her life, by which she existed.

But even in those days the girl had begun to attempt composition of her own. She began to be haunted by the strange tantalizings which are known to the genius of expression. She would be in despair or dullness. Or a muted ecstasy came over her, in which, so high was her vision of the beauty she wanted to embody, she did not dare attempt composition. Everything was hard for her. It was unbearable to remain silent, chilling the music from her heart with duties of the household day; and unbearable to yearn for composition, filled with ineffable impulses which she knew from old would not flower into the singing perfection of art.

Something had happened between their infrequent meetings. Richard had known that, youth as he was; but he had not questioned her closely then or later. She told him that she was not leaving home. The most her willingness could explain was that the music affected her too strongly. She couldn't bear it, and the house was silent for ever, the piano closed, looking like a giant black bier, until it was moved into a storeroom of the rambling house, never opened. And after that again he had not seen her for months. Her mother had had a long illness; Ada had nursed the woman through it, at the same time helping her father and carrying on the household. . . .

Looking at her now, it came to him that Ada Lethen had become that inaccessible music which had tortured her until she could bear it no more. There had been, finally, in her nineteenth year, what the local doctor had called a "nervous breakdown." This had been temporary, and seemed to leave no trace beyond the resignation which baffled her lover now, a sort of nihilism of the emotions, not of the will, which kept her from any new courses, or even acquiescence in the validity of the projects he urged. Yet she seemed strong; her activity dominated the family, which probably, as she said, would fall to pieces without her. It was strength which seemed to be in her soul now, beneath a wild vibrancy to ineffable spiritual intimations he could only guess, and in wonderment reverence.

But again, was it with her as she said, as she believed she felt? She feared that the lives of her parents, her mother, would tumble into ruin if she left them. But did she fear, too, that, lacking their supporting needs, she would collapse, become useless, a recluse, prey once more to music or to love more poignant and devastating still? He would bring all this to light; he would conquer it. He had been gathering his forces during all the months of being apart from her. Now he would test his will, his love for her, his belief in their happiness, test his whole ultimate life and hers. Perhaps his failures, his diversion to the course of ambition, had been a preparation, his own development for the goal which his imagination had held before him in a vision of her.

They had come out of the forest before they knew, and were walking in a by-path near the bank of the river. Their wanderings had transgressed line-fences so vaguely that they did not know whose farm they were crossing. But they knew that the river glided smooth, occasionally revealed below them, the trees were gracious, the vines and hedges veiling. Far ahead of them loomed the top of a broad beech tree, among the slim second growth spared from the axe along the banks. Nearer, its quick leaves glittered before them as though it grew from the middle of the river. And indeed when they came up and stood on the bank opposite the towering old tree, they saw that, far below, it held an isthmus of its own from the river, which was forced to twine about its roots in springtime, but ran several yards away in a sunken bed now. The knoll beneath the trees was high, grassy, sheltered on one hand by a bend in the creek bank, and on the other by two cedars overgrown and joined to form a screen by creeping morning glory vine, which wrapped them to the tips. It was a place for shelter from too rough winds, from sun, and all noise and unquiet they looked into; but there seemed no path leading down to it.

They had scarcely walked fifty feet on along the lane before they met Carson Hymerson, both forks on his shoulder, evidently going home to dinner. The small, thick, stooped man looked at them quickly, suspiciously once, mumbled something, and had passed.

They looked at each other, and Richard Milne smiled.

"He won't be expecting you home for dinner now," Ada said with a soft drawl, "so you'd better come home with me. Never mind," she said with sudden decision as he began to excuse himself. "I want you to meet Mother, and it's no inconvenience."

His acceptance was curiously tentative, tacit. "You seem to know Carson."

She laughed a little. "Yes, but I wonder whether I do. One thinks one knows this one and that one, when, if one did, things would be different; there would be no flaws in intercourse."

"Obviously here there are. But don't you think that it is possible to know people too well for their comfort and yours?"

"Perhaps, if you know them without sympathy. But then if you didn't sympathize you couldn't know anyone perfectly. Could you? And if you did know a person perfectly you would be compelled to sympathize with him."

"Perhaps." Richard Milne was not tempted to explore this syllogism. "Still, people don't like to be understood. Not really. Not too well; and perhaps it is fortunate I don't understand Carson Hymerson. But he does cause me to speculate."

"I think my father does him, too," she said with an intonation of sadness. "If only such people would resign themselves not to understand. They seem to think that since my father is what they call 'queer,' they are licensed for any means to attain their ends, the petty ends of trickery. They do manage to bother him; it can't be denied. I can't see why they should attempt to do so, or what they hold against him. I suppose to see anyone unhappy arouses a sadistic tendency in coarser minds." Her voice trembled.

"Ada," broke in Richard Milne, his tones sharp and yet heavy, "you just tell me when anything overt – but, of course, nothing can happen, save by the rarest mischance. I'd just like to see them bother you." Ada looked up at the savageness of his tone. A thwarted anger struggled within him at the thought that this girl should be forced to consider such a trifle as he denominated the rest of the community, the rest of the world.

Her eyes met his intense gaze, then looked away and filled, while she caught her breath. "Dear boy . . ." she murmured. "Nothing's going to happen."

"Promise me you will," he insisted.

"Yes. I shall be glad of any help you can give." She spoke in the steady tones of one unwilling to reveal an invisible burden.

"Ada!" He stopped, unsatisfied, as though uncertain of what he wished to say to her, or of how he was to say it. "You don't seem to realize my right – haven't I earned it? – to want to protect you, in all the years you've ruled my life." He laughed shakily. "Why, my dear, I wouldn't be here. . . . Love is like –"

"Hush!"

"Like an intermittent fever." He had stopped in his preoccupation.

"Hush!" She stepped back toward him, taking his hand. "We are nearly there. Let's talk about – anything – dinner, until you can eat it! You're too late for the locust blossoms." She waved her hand above them.

They walked along together beneath the high, grey-barked trees with their fine, small leaves. The upper branches showed dead, broken off straight and blunt on the tops of the trees, and would have been even more conspicuous by contrast when the great white blooms of locust were interspersed among them.

When the pair reached the road the dust was deeper, but they saw that their shoes already had been covered by the deposit on the grasses of the lanes. In noonday silence and glare the river road was like a snake twining into the shade of the weeds, as it wended below uneven elms and clumps of wild apple, sumach, and elderberry in the fence corners. The road made Richard silent, perhaps with a memory of his walk along it the afternoon before and the night before, perhaps with the memories of earlier times.

SEVEN

U nder this white glare of sunlight the Lethen place was appreciably less ominous and more dilapidated than it had appeared the previous night. The very trees edging the lawn at the road and along the drive seemed veterans recalling many storms. Rust-coloured needles and rotting cones were strewn beneath the evergreens in arcs which encroached upon the uneven and tufted grass. The brick gables of the house above the Virginia creeper were bleached and eroded of mortar like the face of a harridan washed of paint in the morning light. The roof, dirt-coloured shingles edged with green, looked water-soaked, and as they walked toward it Richard Milne could see a thread of sky through the top of an ornate, tall, ochre chimney.

"Your house doesn't seem to change," he remarked, grasping at symbolism as he spoke, "but still it does. It's becoming more dilapidated and worn, more forsaken-looking every year."

"Ah, forsaken." She laughed. "At any rate you don't say, as almost anyone else would, that it looks smaller than your memories of it."

"No, not smaller. Nothing connected with it could dwindle." He brought the implication to light.

Ada Lethen sighed, and they walked up the damp and shady lane in silence, turned across the unfenced lawn, and stood on the patch of grass, which was turning yellow from exposure to the sun, before the veranda.

"Come right in," said Ada, as he hesitated on the sagging veranda. "It's time I got dinner. Or would you rather wait here?"

He shook his head, and they went into a front room of indeterminate size and character, until his eyes became used to the dimness. Vague huge patterns adorned the wallpaper; the carpet was green, with great yellow scrollings. A sewing-machine stood in one corner, and in another stood a wood-burning stove without a pipe. Above was the hole in the ceiling through which it would have to reach the chimney, and glancing up, Richard Milne fancied that he heard a hasty stirring, silenced at once. Ada had retreated to the back of the house, after having murmured something about her mother. The young man crossed his knees and prepared to look as much more at ease than he felt, as the impending presence of Mrs. Lethen would allow.

Until now he had not noticed the table, perhaps because, directly before him, it was too obvious. A large square dining-table, covered with a dark chenille cloth extending in shadowy pattern almost to the floor. On the cloth rested two large bowls, bearing each three bulbs of white narcissus, all in flower, and nicely arranged with the tallest in the middle of each bowl. The brilliance of these flowers, hard as flame for all their whiteness, seemed to diffuse a certain radiance throughout the dim room, with its two windows latticed by the creeping vine. The window-sills themselves, he noticed, each bore more bulbs, and the sewing-machine in the corner must have had one, but for the necessity of use, for it was opened, and on a chair beside it stood still another vase.

A gaunt, pale woman entered at this moment, and it was with something like terror in his surprise that Richard rose, facing her haggard and piercing eyes, even as Ada appeared behind her.

She grasped his hand, holding it high and limply for an instant, and then dropped it. Something made Ada speak, as though the two were strangers newly met.

"Mr. Milne has consented to stay to dinner with us, but I'm afraid he'll have a little wait, for I've just put the potatoes on to boil. I spent too long on my walk, it seems. But we'll be alone."

The woman peered into his face quickly, but without seeming to have heard her daughter's last words. Then with a sharp glance aside she took a chair, laughing.

"Yes, you'll have to see to dinner, now you've said you would."

"I've every sympathy with her intentions," remarked Milne, "and I'm sure she can feel for us, since she has been out developing an appetite of her own." He tried to put understanding and support into his smiling attitude toward the girl. She turned away to the kitchen, leaving the door open.

Silence seemed to deaden the air of the room like a gas. There was nothing to be said to this lady, and the impression of the first seconds that she was an enemy returned to him, became conscious, so that he watched her critically.

Her dress was not old-fashioned: timeless rather, so that it would have seemed to become her in any age or scene: a long black skirt, a white shirt-waist. Her hair was white, and though brushed straight back, so abundant that it seemed a tangled mass. Her face was almost equally colourless, except for black eyebrows, dark burnt-out eyes. Her mouth kept up a constant movement of mood or, he considered, of calculated foiling of decipherment.

Half purposely he waited, feeling that she might be driven to utterance. What things in her soul! A feeling of pity arose upon his reverence of the mystery of life. His eyes roved hither and thither about the room, as though unaccustomed to it, then, as if in resolved defiance, rested upon the narcissi. She opened her lips.

"Look at them!" She extended her hand, smooth and well-kept. "Look at them. Aren't they beautiful?" She laughed abruptly, as at an understatement so grotesque. "Beautiful!"

"Your narcissi are very nice," observed Richard Milne with sedate inflections, "and you have a good number of them too!" He did not veil the acid of his smile, behind firm eyes.

Her silence became remote as she looked at the flowers, then she seemed to return to him, and finally she said, as though satirically:

"They're worth coming a long way to see, aren't they, Mr. Milne?"

He had to own himself beaten at the futile and childish game of discomfiture – what he called the feeling which gave rise to alarmed pity, carrying anxiety into his mind. Candour was better than such obvious perversity. There would have to be a reckoning, and he struck, with a directness which surprised them both.

"Mrs. Lethen," he contended in deliberate tones, "don't you find something more beautiful in the souls of people about you than in these flowers? Something warmer at least, that concerns you, your own fate and your happiness, rather than a momentary pleasure of the eyes. Are you sure that you

67

have not raised up an idol? Are you not likely to waken some time and find that everything vital in your life is gone, and there is left only these wilted flowers to mock you? What of the happiness of your daughter? Have you ever thought that Ada deserved your support, all your effort now, to gain the happiness which the world, which life is saving for her, and which for reasons which you know it may be hard for her to discover? It is possible to look across the fields of everyday life to some mirage of mountains, longing to be there, and to find after years that one's limbs are too worn even to gather the valley flowers of reality. And then the mirage dissolves; you are left with nothing who might have had all the sweets of reality without the empty yearning of thwarted longing for unseizable beauty. But how empty and cold is such beauty without the part fulfilled by others. Think how wonderfully different Ada's life would be, and your own. Sacrifice is the badge of motherhood, and the honour of it finer than any flower."

Labelling himself a prig, he was consciously letting himself be carried away, so that, while at first his feeling had driven him to words, now the words were cumulating, carrying forward his emotion.

"The world! Beauty! The soul! Idols!" Mrs. Lethen's white face laughed without interest or surprise at this long outburst. "Yes. I have erected an idol, and since it gives more satisfaction to my days, leavens them better than the clods of this dull life can, who is to say me nay? If they give me the love everything and everyone else denies me, what then?" She paused, as though surprised at this revelation coming uncalled from her lips. "Sacrifice. How like a man," she murmured, while her face took on a marble quietude, staring now at the hole in the ceiling. Then abruptly she rose and passed into the kitchen.

"Excuse me," she dropped in a perfect, conventionally polite tone at the door, which she was closing. "I should help her."

"Indeed, yes!"

The young man remained plunged in thought, apart from his consciousness of the house of his dreams and forebodings. He did not raise his eyes; he was feeling that he had always been there, as Ada had – living for himself her life – until the girl reappeared and called him to the meal.

She was changed. He saw it while she enumerated casually the excuses necessary for her extempore cooking, the tardiness and lack of conveniences. He paid little heed to the neat, painted, and oilclothed kitchen in which the table was set, with Mrs. Lethen opposite him and Ada pouring tea at the head. A kettle sang diminuendo over a wood fire in a dull, huge stove, but a window was open above the fourth side of the table. Upon the sill a pad of fly poison floated in water among a few dead flies. He spoke pleasantly and generally at first. Ada was preoccupied with serving the dinner, and Mrs. Lethen maintained, of purpose, he saw, a watchful silence.

As he talked and the meal progressed he became aware of an obscene, unreasonable foreboding, and began to struggle with a sense that he was talking against time, like a man waiting to be taken to the gallows, who must conceal the fact. Ada replied to his remarks with consideration, as though weighing the literal meaning of each of them. The older woman's face, he now saw, was more fleshy than he had supposed, and more paste-like in colour. Her mouth was rayed with wrinkles gathering and slackening. With her chief attention on her food, she regarded him from time to time with a detachment almost amounting to hauteur. The oppression increased upon him, while with desperate inquiry he cajoled his strange impulse to rise and be gone. Surely it was all nothing. He had been recalling aloud old-time friends and neighbours, then:

"Mr. Lethen is not at home to-day?" he asked the face opposite him, almost unaware of speaking at all, as one might unwittingly strike a mortal blow in a mêlée of combat.

The attitude of Ada Lethen gave him a feeling of having impudently blurted like a schoolboy. It was so conspicuously tense that he did not heed her mother for the moment.

"If you are really anxious to see my father, he will be at home to-night, or almost any time after that." It was as though he had been to Ada some stranger meddlesome in personal matters, some tradesman, a dealer come to buy a load of cattle or to sell her father a hay-loader.

"Unfortunate," he murmured.

His own ire rose.

"I had naturally hoped to see him, but, of course, I am not giving up hope."

The two women said nothing. Richard, not to be drawn into conventional insincerities of manner, much less of fact, resigned himself almost to monosyllables until the end of the meal, and found himself once more in the sitting-room with Mrs. Lethen, whom he asked if he might smoke. He had still to put in time until Ada should have dispatched her duties. Talk as he might, the woman stared alternately at the narcissi and at himself. Finally he was driven out to the veranda, and after waiting there another half-hour in a mounting uneasiness he walked over the lawn, already shaded pointedly along the western side by the row of evergreens. Returning, he found a stillness which seemed to bespeak a house deserted. At last he heard a step within and, going to the door, addressed Mrs. Lethen: would she speak to Ada?

The very appearance of the girl, her quick step, look of concern, was reassuring to his now obviously absurd fear, which had been tantalizing, like that of a man who has lost a precious stone in the grass. In the relief and gratitude of having her before him again, as though she had escaped who knew what occult fate, he was made sure of all that he had doubted, and her bearing seemed to tell him that, instead of anything coming between them unaware, they were more subtly linked than before.

"What is it?"

He looked at her reproachfully, with a smile that made light of all he had been feeling, a smile which was to take away the embarrassment she must share. "What should it be? Do you want me to go away without seeing you?"

"Yes."

"But, Ada! What's the matter? What has come over you since I came?" He saw his worst fears realized, and himself put against one of those unforeseeable psychic debacles as intangible as they are overpowering, and as irremediable as insidious.

"I don't like the attitude you take toward my parents." Ada spoke calmly.

"And I don't like the attitude they take toward you," he answered in a flare of anger. "Nor to me either. I thought you could make allowance for at least that."

"Your course then seems obvious." Her tone was unfathomable, without feeling. She might have been torturing him, though he fancied that if torturing herself she was delighting in the agony.

"My course is not obvious, but it will be definite, when I've decided. I've had about enough of this."

She made no reply, and so uncertain had everything become that he wondered whether in this he should see hope or forbearance which was more strongly entrenched than active repugnance; she did not ask him to go.

"What did your mother say in the kitchen?" he demanded. "What did she say about me?"

She shook her head slowly, looking far away over the fields, to the bright forest splotched with dark shade. There was no indecision apparent in her air, yet to Richard's vexation it was as though she did not know what she was doing, what she wanted. With an effort he eschewed forcible expression of this feeling of his; in a situation which seemed to him to demand the utmost care of reasonableness and good sense, these qualities appeared to have deserted Ada Lethen, and he was further angered by the abruptness with which he discovered them measurably lost to himself; when he should have risen to an occasion he was ready for any wild and final word or action.

"Let us go for a walk. You can't see things straight here, Ada; I can explain. Come."

He had never seen her more beautiful, in poise of foot and head. Her eyes were no longer sad, but bright with some enigma beyond his conception, wide, unfathomable, maddening:

"No, thank you."

Fearing himself, he turned and was gone. He would not say never to return to that house.

EIGHT

S he had spoken, and he had pretended to accept what she said. He could scarcely convince even himself that there was any use of hoping, or of staying here. He could love her, with a love which should have moved mountains, and blown trivial obstacles from them as sand is swept across a beach, which should have caused happiness as the air of a valley is changed, charged with sunlight. But as for being effectively moved by these considerations, she might have been a worn-out stump in such a valley, on such a beach. What balked him, what finally enraged him, was not the feeling that she did not return his love, or the difficulty of convincing her that she loved him, but the fact that love could make so little difference. He had found exaltation and in his darkest despair had taken consolation from thinking that he was to learn what love alone could do, and he thought he saw now that it could do nothing when circumstances and temperaments conspired to cause a deadlock.

Nothing, nothing to be done, his mind repeated, and he did not know how he put in the rest of the day, the afternoon and evening. The Hymersons seemed to take it for granted that he should be preoccupied, revisiting his old haunts. It was an effort to recall the day of the week and month. No mail pursued him, he was cut off from his old world, and no work could be undertaken; no reading reminded him of either work or world.

As time passed he discovered that he was curiously thrust back into a self, an existence which he had thought to forget with boyhood. Sitting on a corn-cultivator in rough farm clothes, musing at the end of a row, he admitted to himself that it was not the circumstances of the present, his vacation, or any plan which held him. Days were following each other, and though they were futile, when he recalled their manifest summer beauty he lingered, postponed deciding to go. Before long, tired of the feeling of a spectator while every hour he became more a part of that former life, he had volunteered to join the Hymersons in their farm work.

"Well, I kind of thought from the start you was sensible that way, not scairt of getting your hands soiled," Carson told him. "We got an extra team all right, unless you'd rather use the hoe."

Any kind of work which would be of use, Richard assured him, would do, but he preferred a job of driving horses at first. Since no change in the terms of lodging was mentioned, the farmer was well satisfied, and disposed even to make a confidant of his guest, to become intimate with him. As opportunity arose Carson told him of all the wrongs he was suffering from his neighbours, particularly from Mr. Lethen; the misunderstanding of his motives when he told people how things should and could be run; and prophecies of what would happen where his advice was disregarded. And Richard would lean against the dusty wall while evenings passed, interjecting the necessary rejoinders, keeping his thoughts from wandering far. Or he helped Carson with the milking, tying the cow's tail by its longest hair about the animal's hind leg.

Arvin Hymerson had soon given up interest in the new dispensation, baffled by the city man's apparent listlessness. He spent most evenings in the village store, which was a source of audible deprecation to his father. "He didn't use to be that way," the latter declared with a puzzled smile. "He didn't use to be the kind to waste time like that. I can't figure out what's got into him lately. He don't seem to have no interest in home ties, somehow." Milne was only surprised that Arvin had not been "this way" long ago. He was aware of a sympathetic reaching-out from the young man, but his own calloused and languid response did not add enough to serve as the basis of companionship. It seemed to be as unnecessary that they should be friends as that they should not be friends.

Usually silent and equable, the two were well-matched to set off the garrulity of Carson, who at noon would glance at yesterday's paper, and start ridiculing the evolutionary theory, at the time coming in for much publicity. Mrs. Hymerson, by way of maintaining a balance, sought to defend it with equal unreason: "Why, Pa, you know there's negroes in Africa a lot like monkeys."

"Not me. When them ginks start talking about evolution to me, I just got to say, 'Look at Paul. Do they build better men than Paul nowadays?'" Arvin smiled without seeking the attention of Richard.

As day passed after day Milne knew himself deadened in them, carefully following such routine as was discoverable, trying to work out a programme which would account for all of his waking hours. He rose early, though once at first Carson Hymerson deferentially waived the right of calling him;

harnessed the team, which had been curried the night before; ate breakfast to the equally inane jocularity or resentment of his host's talk, and the almost surprised taciturnity of Mrs. Hymerson and Arvin; hitched the team to the cultivator or the mower, if he were not hoeing potatoes or pitching hay. Through the long hours of morning and afternoon he attempted participation in the ever-wonderfully oblivious pageantry of nature: sunlight, birds, greying green of oats, stylized symmetry of waxing corn-hills; ripening amber ponds of wheat; in breezes for a damp brow, rain to give a half-day's respite. He felt that he had been part of this for ever.

Still a general enveloping indifference almost imposed upon him the illusion that something did hold him there. It was to go farther, coupled with the monotonous routine, until he found that to himself he was at times that earlier uncouth boy, for whom nothing was sure, not even his own hope or his smothered longing to get away into the world. He scarcely remembered his late life in the city, his books, his dealings with editors and publishers, film companies, and a return there seemed inconceivable. Only with a start, perhaps lying on a load of hay, through which the rumble and boom of the wagon and the trotting horses smote his ears, would he return to Richard Milne, and the courage once more to admit that what held him there would be resolved this time or lost for ever. That alone was enough to make him hesitate, and again he would be driven back by reluctance of the test, never giving up the certainty that years might elapse, and his former interests drop from him one after another, but he would go, when he did go, with Ada Lethen, conclusively and for ever.

Her part in his life, he looked back and saw, had been of a strong growth with his ambition and his bent for expression. And when those had taken him to the city against his will, where he had slaved and managed until his first books came out, and at the same time he had obtained a foothold in the advertising field, he still thought of no other woman. He was not long in discovering that his need was not physical simply, and convinced of this he was prepared to allow himself a latitude which he saw in the lives of people around him, sure that he would never become engrossed. He had no leisure for that, he told himself and once or twice a friend or two; and he felt the need of no emancipation.

They would have smiled with irony had they known; freedom was impossible for him. The first vantage-place attained, he found himself back, besieging her inaccessible ears. Nothing could exhaust his patience, ever in imminence, as it seemed, of breaking. She had become the core of his life, of all his intimate work, the concern of his hours, so that he could not write an eloquent sentence, see a fair morning, or step aside from danger, without her face. He could never forget holding her in his arms, and it was with enormous surprise that he would rouse himself in the seething flotsam of the city.

His second return – with unregarded laurels – had been as vain as the first, as all former time; and when writing and his sense of the city had engulfed him again he declared that he could never go back. Yet, with a finality of faith he would willingly have relegated to poetry, he seemed thrust into a fate of unrelieved constancy. And, since he could not bear the thought of flight, here he was back – rebuffed as he had been before, wounded by a futility alien to the remainder of his world.

Always her outward passivity had matched his patience. Yet, in a tone of her voice, a look, he surprised all yearning and compunction at his averted despair; in her unexpected pronouncement of his name he had detached tiny glints, something more – like sight of a goal – that seemed an index of her heart, that dreamed a little, while it seemed to rest in sleep. Though Ada Lethen and the part she played with him were the most familiar things to his mind, they formed its greatest mystery – more profound because part of the mystery was himself.

Because he was part of the mystery he wondered at it the more. He had two months before him in which it seemed he meant to do nothing except indulge his sense of desperation and his sudden attack of listlessness – though within him the purpose still held to achieve a different finality. So he told himself, with a conscious effort to rouse himself to that purpose once more. Time, after all, was effecting changes in the one thing which had appeared changeless in his life. He would not have settled here to this dumb inaction a few years ago; he would have betaken himself to the city, anywhere away from the scene of his repulse. The thought held frightening possibilities. What was this business making of him? Unaccustomed, his mind was fascinated by the question. There must have been changes in him before this, which others had noticed, which he would begin to see as time passed. He would become after all a man essentially estranged from life, at least from the world, a romantic figure of absurd incompleteness, an unadjusted person, if successful in art, which does not demand normality, "a queer stick." All for what? "He lost a woman," one-time friends would say.

These doubts of himself were not allayed when he thought of the change in Ada Lethen beyond the sameness of circumstance and the timelessness of her beauty. That would be stamped more finely with the years; she would always be Ada, but these would make her in the end just a woman, an "old maid" with a temper! Perhaps she would be as nearly commonplace as that . . . but a denying flood, impressions of her ways and charms, swept through his memory. She never would be like other women. Yet there was some new recognition of the hardness of life which she had been forced in the interval of his absence to meet – or was forced now to consider. Perhaps in himself . . . he had not gone quite unscathed; he was beginning to know himself for a different man in these quiet, memory-haunted fields. He roused and started the horses down another row of corn.

But after consideration he rejected as self-flattery the thought that her petulance had been a reflex of the emotion he desired in her. Nor was it pique. It was love of her mother, of her whole past life, which spoke when the mother came into clash with the man who loved her. She felt smothered by circumstance, yes; she loved him, perhaps; but that molten penetralia in her soul had never crystallized to jewelled hardness shining through the ponderous, iron-fretted doors, "portion and parcel of the dreadful past." She might even know that she loved him; but if it had been a slow growth, that love had never become the flame of her being, he thought, as his rare love had been – to burn from her the coils of duty and pity and half-forgotten hatred which bound her – to make her follow wherever he should lead.

Yet he recalled moments. . . . Perhaps, perhaps there was a centre of storm in her which, caught up with his own, in time would make, if necessary, an upheaval in the lives of everyone about them, once it had arisen. What held them back; what held him back? Until now he had trusted to reasoning and delicacies of aspiration, longing and intellectualized passion. Now futility whispered to him crudely. . . . What means did other men take?

He would not admit that he was baffled; but every day saw him sunk more deeply into an inertia distinct from his revived interest in farm ways, moderately healthy spirits and appetite. He did not know that he went about with the air of one sentenced irretrievably, yet bearing up with thoroughbred reserve. His syndicate had allowed him the holiday, and he assumed that there was no use in his going elsewhere to spend it – in going anywhere now. Still, his condition forbade inaction, and a part taken in the farmer's routine put him back into that state of wilfully resigned hopeless longing of his early years. So that after the first few days he felt that Ada Lethen was miles away, out of reach, and each day added its weight to his sense that he must not go to see her, to his inability to visualize himself in such an attitude again.

Where was his appreciated success, his poise between introspection and enterprise, which had made him the poetical novelist and one of the most adept writers of mail-order advertising matter of his generation? The years which had laid the foundation of that surety, in health and resolute patience with hard circumstance, had returned upon him, and he seemed a callow youth daunted by a now unapproachable ideal, eating his heart out unwittingly before the suddenly comprehended difficulty of life. He felt that he had never worn anything but the overalls and shirt in which he was cultivating corn.

The afternoon was sultry, but the breeze played with rasping corn-leaves throughout the dark field, and he rested his team beside the road before another plunge among the dense growth. In a sudden revelation of his impotence he sat with hands uplifted on the handles of the cultivator as in a gesture of awe or beseeching, his head lowered, eyes regarding the dusty grass of the headland as they had overseen the passing hills of corn as he drove along them.

An automobile shot past with a flying streamer of dust, and the people in the tonneau turned to look back at him. He smiled grimly as they vanished down the worming river road, and in a second his thoughts had returned upon him in a wave.

There was a soft clop-clop in the dust, and a buggy, faintly rattling, approached. Beneath the open top sat a bronzed, heavy-featured man and a slight, thin-clad boy. As Richard Milne nodded he recognized Wallace Bender, a former neighbour.

"Hello, Dick, old boy!" the man shouted cordially. "Back on the land, eh? Poetry played out, I suppose! Well, that's all right for a side line," Bender continued in a confidential tone, wagging his head, "but for a living you got to get down to farming; that's the sure thing to stick to." The boy looked on, curious.

Richard laughed, and inquired regarding his old neighbour's family, and when they had passed the time of day and he went on cultivating he was surprised at the resentment which filled his breast. It was as though he really concurred in Bender's appraisal. The latter, after all, must have detected something in his bearing which told of defeat. That it was not in the material battle was Milne's disadvantage. But he was unappeased, overtaken by a rage for not having told him – the crabbed skinflint with his criterion of a village mortgage-holder – how much in money he had made in the past year. But the other would not have believed. And though Milne told himself how little it mattered, his discomfort was unabated; until he laughed at these new qualms of self-esteem, the general absurd upheaval in himself. . . . Perhaps after all Ada Lethen had spoken from an inner discord properly encouraging.

"Nothing will resolve doubt but action," Goethe had said it. He would go and see Ada Lethen again. He would watch every ripple between their minds; he would not lose control of his emotions this time. But a sad private smile of incredulity met the thought, while a symbolic rhythmic monotony of corn brushed his knees. His mouth hardened. He would tell her once for all – but what was the use of telling her anything? She was in possession of all the determining factors which should move her. They did not suffice. Surely she comprehended his point of view, perfectly sympathized with it, supported it with her reason. In vain. Hers was an obsession with duty. Let her have time to ponder the value of her loyalty, he thought with quick savagery. Let her wait and think things out. But his anger melted; he recalled that she had surely done so, surely had had time. He was in a maze, helpless.

Yet a miracle was possible, and perhaps one was happening now. He could hope that the passing of years would be compressed in sensation into days, and she should see herself alone, prey to memories and the squalid, tacit recriminations of her parents. And after that, nothingness, more memories changed from a torture to her only solace. Unless he lived still . . . and found his way back.

He looked up when the horses stopped, and saw that he had come to the end of the row, which from youthful habitude he had followed accurately, without injury to a stalk of corn. He was still the prey of conflicting emotions. He did not know what to do with himself. Action – to fight. He should have liked to catch Bender again to lecture him on his small-spiritedness . . . though he saw the absurdity of accepting that man as a representative of the outer world – of which a considerable portion would be wondering what had become of him, and which had a regard for him sufficiently favourable. He was allowing this matter to disturb him, was acting as though nothing else existed but these few people, and as though there were nothing to be done but to accept their point of view, their limitations, and ineffectiveness. But something must happen. Things could not go on in this way. For weeks he had felt an oppression amounting at times to physical sensation.

There was his writing. But he expected the galley proofs of his latest book in a couple of weeks; and he had permitted the lack of typewriter and reference works to keep him from the beginning of even the first draft of his next one. He had determined upon spending his summer here, and he would do so, though every day put him further at the mercy of the woman who had waited at the completion of every page he had ever written, whose imagined wonder only the most intense compacted inspiration could dim. Even the utterly sapped weariness of mind and body after long creative effort hardly could make his longing tolerable – inspiriting so that he could bend to more effort again.

In a bright, fevered dream, with tangential flying wraiths of hope, so had the years, the best years, gone. While each book became more monumental than the last, he promised himself that the end of each would mark his return, his finally triumphant return, his bearing-off of that girl, never to see this confined place again. She feared, she feared. But for him there was more security even in flight, and any place in the world represented less of a danger to their love than this sheltered countryside in a remote part of Canada.

Well, if ever she consented, there would be no delay, no hesitation. How poignantly had every step been printed in his mind long ago, so that whenever the suggestion came he busied himself automatically with travellers' letters of credit, calculations of railway and steamship lines, hotels. . . . It was still impossible to believe that they could rest there happily, even in the definitive achievement of their love. Even if the old people – died.

No, they'd go away. They would be like children, happily lost babes in the woods of this wondrous world. At last the grip upon him would loosen: he would do none but his best creative work, a flowering of unbelievable peace, of immense happiness. They would look back upon these people, these fields in the way they should be regarded; perhaps at last, by the operation of the irony in life, they would seek out others like them. They would look back with removed pity, even with the quality of affection one has for an old dog dead long years ago. What was memory for but that? Yes, it was possible, he smiled to himself bitterly, that they could yet see something of benignance in even these tortured times. . . .

Perhaps the fault lay all in himself, not – as he had always felt – a strong man. Was it a lack of inclination over some deeper lack? Didn't he want her badly enough? He had seen enough of men that it profited him nothing to ask himself how others would have acted in his circumstances. He might – but his mind recoiled. He could not connect such impulses with the defined image of Ada Lethen. And since in the world he had had his opportunities and found no freedom, he did not give much credence to the physical side of his love. It seemed to be something deeper than his desires, than his will, like a spell cast upon his mind while it had been forming. He could never find freedom but in complete enslavement.

No, bitterly as he sought something to be blamed for all this, even something in himself, he could not admit a fundamental lack of passion, not even in Ada Lethen. He would rather indict this oppressive atmosphere, this time and place, which smothered spontaneity and natural virtue. Perhaps it really had ruined Ada? . . . And reason told him at the same time that that was a recession to adolescent standards, that there was as much freedom anywhere as one could take. He invoked all the operose sophistries of his generation.

"Get up there!" He slapped the horses savagely with the lines as he turned them awkwardly round. He was doing little. Musing thus at the ends of the field, he was scarcely vindicating the intention of service to Hymerson which he had professed tacitly, whether or not any were owing.

NINE

The horses raised heads and ears suddenly, and the young man, looking too, saw a strange sight. The cornfield abutted on the line fence between the Hymerson and Lethen places, and over the fence was a gloom of trees, dark even now beyond a clearing minaretted by mulleins. The shadowed oaks and maples seemed darkened thickly, and even with their flourish of green, somehow old and cool, wintry. And before them, in the clearing among the slender spires of mullein, stood a human figure.

Never since beginning work in this field had Milne's subconscious alertness given way, as though some time, among the green, he would descry the face of Ada Lethen, calling him. . . . Though nothing of the sort could happen; she would see him from among the bush and avoid him, unless . . . he were to consider himself dreaming more wildly than ever.

It was not she. The figure was strangely forlorn, as though strayed there by chance from some indefinitely remote quarter, an alien. It was hatless, with straggling grey hair, and advanced to him almost as though subjectively cringing; suggesting the same motives as a stray dog.

It was a man, who appeared to sidle around stumps and mulleins, fallen logs, a huge ant-city, without noticing such obstacles, or even Richard Milne, upon whom he was nevertheless intent as though looking through him. The face was long and grey, with cleaving perpendicular lines below, and level ones on the forehead criss-crossed by the straggling hair. The figure was not so much stooped as attenuated, slighter, so that it seemed at first as tall as in former times. Arrived at the fence, he leaned against the topmost rail as though there was no danger that his weight would displace it, and gazed earnestly with slate-grey eyes into the young man's face.

"Good day, Mr. Lethen." Richard Milne spoke with a recollected sort of serene severity. His hands twitched upon the levers of the cultivator. The other did not reply, but gazed at the young man with an almost entreating intentness. There was indeed something dog-like in his haggard eyes, and his shoulders seemed twistedly sagging, knobbled by heavy braces over the khaki shirt – store clothes, machine-made, as those of other farmers seldom were. His dejection, however, spoke an indifference to all details of the sort which gave him an air of natural things and weathered objects, as though he had never been beneath a roof within memory.

These matters, and the silence, gave Richard Milne an exasperation which, as he was half-conscious, transposed the natural pity following on a shock of recognition. His mood stiffened as he told himself that everything was the old fellow's own fault, in part at least. All the pent-up bitterness of years found vent in a monosyllable, while he tugged at the lines as it were to turn the team about:

"Well?"

"You are Alma Milne's son, aren't you?"

The gentle plangency of the tone, the words, surprised Richard into his natural courteous consideration. He had almost forgotten that he had been an orphan from early years, and had not thought ever to be saluted in that manner again. Memories of childhood and a dark country back of that, with weeping at a black winter funeral, stirred him.

"Ada, my daughter, has told me about you," went on the tired voice. "You've changed a little, or it seems so to me, since your last visit." He meant the visit before last. They had not met, Richard recalled, at the time of his last repulse, "I understand you are to be congratulated on very creditable work. I'm glad," he added simply, gazing about at the woods as though the scene of that work had put him forward to thank the artist in its behalf. Richard almost laughed with a mixture of incredulity, thwarted hostility, impatience, smothered pity.

"Thank you, Mr. Lethen. What can I do for you?"

The brusqueness did not cause the old man to change attitude or expression, yet he seemed to consult an inward necessity whether it would force him on in the face of this hard unconcern.

"I hardly know how to put it," he ventured. "You are helping Carson just now, and I don't want to be bearing tales against him like this. But it seems like there's nothing else to be done. You must have noticed his attitude. And I was wondering whether you couldn't do anything to straighten things out."

"I might," agreed Milne readily, "if I could see in what way it affected me." His feeling of the earlier afternoon had died down, but he felt that he must play with the old man a little before descending to that store of vehemence he had at times consciously been keeping for such an opportunity as this occasion offered. Wrath distilled in verbal form, since any other was out of the question. He had long desired to tell Mr. and Mrs. Lethen his opinion of such a course as they followed.

"It means everything," the old man was saying earnestly, "everything to me, to get this straightened out. Surely there's a way."

"Are you sure now that it wouldn't be necessary to make Carson over for that, as well as, perhaps, yourself?" Richard enjoyed abominably and delicately the brightening and the fall in the old man's look.

"Of course, to come right down to it at once, it's us, our own fault. You can blame us both. It's his way, and it's my being what I am. But still there is no need of things coming to such a pass. . . ."

"Between neighbours, eh?" The tone was ironical almost to bitterness, but the bitterness was half with Richard's own perversity, for in that moment he recalled the way – romantic it seemed to the real of the present – in which his writing had glossed over such differences, with all the life of which they formed part.

The old man glanced at him. "Yes, between neighbours. When we've always got along, I may say, perfectly. When I first settled here as a young man I used to compliment myself on having such good neighbours. They were kind of backward about associating, but awfully obliging, lend you anything you asked for. My father used to say it was worthwhile living here just to have such good neighbours. Then things changed little by little, the younger fellows came along, like Carson, and somehow they seemed to see things differently. They kept away more than ever. Not shy, they weren't. They seemed to take pride in being independent, I suppose they called it."

"In other words, their fathers had to swallow your learning and possibly your manner and means, and the sons' teeth are edged with an inferiority complex. But to what pass is it that things, as you say, are coming?"

"Things couldn't go much farther between neighbours," Mr. Lethen assured him again. "I had to go in to see my lawyer, the other day, and he says it's nothing which should go to court."

Milne's impatience began to escape him. "Apparently you are sure you want trouble, or you would not go to a lawyer. If matters have gone to that stage, I'm sure I can't see there's anything but for you to go ahead until you both get your fill of dissension, and the costs connected with it –" He stopped abruptly. Words seemed to burn his tongue for utterance, but he would hold his peace until the man had shot his bolt. Then for an accounting, an understanding from first to last.

"But you see I had to go to see my lawyer, since Hymerson has filed a suit against me. The only thing now is to try to get it settled out of court. It puzzles me – it puzzles me still. I can't see what he should have against me."

"And, if you care to tell me, what is he suing you for?"

"For my land."

The old man spoke with such simplicity, as though expecting his hearer to comprehend, that Milne wondered whether he had heard correctly.

"Your land!" he exclaimed, surprised out of his posing. "What title has Carson Hymerson to your land?"

"None that will stand in court. But that is another matter, scarcely relevant. There's a mortgage – I've had one for years – against the farm. He has got hold of the mortgage, and he has always wanted the farm."

"And your lawyer tells you that his claim won't stand.

That is most fortunate for you." The sedate blandness of incomprehension was part of his design; the unhappy are the most cruel of people.

Mr. Lethen went on with a patience which ignored this. His brows rose into wrinkles in his hair. "No, it only postpones my difficulty. It's not necessary for him to win. The expense if I lose will be enough to put me where I can't wiggle – as Carson himself told me. I guess it's true enough. After the lawsuit, even if the court doesn't give him judgement, holding the mortgage, he'll be able to sell me out. He could now, if he only knew. I might as well tell him that." The voice rose in bitterness. "But after the lawsuit there won't even be public opinion to hinder him. That goes by the board when you get into trouble. Then he can say that I'd do as much to him if I could, that I tried, and so on. People that don't know me would believe it. He has his standing as an officer in farmers' organizations and the like."

"Well," intervened Milne in strong, deliberate tones, "that is not as it may be assumed now. It would not appear safe to generalize until after the event." He said this as gravely as though he more than half meant it.

"I tell you, Mr. Milne," the thin-faced man cried in sudden passion, "it has got me going. I don't know what I am going to do. There must be something, some way. I thought at first it's not possible that such a thing could happen. But it appears to be possible all right. I guess I'll have to admit I've been worrying about it. . . ." His manner made the young man think of Ada Lethen – strangely, since never had there been this fire of instancy in the speech of the daughter. And after there came her gentle smile, in a way which appeared to expect that no one knew he had had any other cause for worry throughout his life.

Richard Milne's hand stilled the lines upon the backs of his horses, and he plunged into reflection. It was only after a moment that he recalled the wisdom of not being hasty of belief in everything told him. There should be limits to the recognized irresponsibility of Carson. And it was strange that the old man Lethen should appeal to him, to one so far – and in such manner – from being a stranger. Perhaps it was an attempt at forestalling him. Was it merely a grotesque manner of broaching acquaintanceship on the part of this weird old man with the haunted eyes? Yes, those eyes had seen trouble enough in this life, Milne knew, more than is usually given in the lot of man. More, it occurred to him, strangely, than his own were likely to see; his own trouble seemed temporary and simple. But perhaps those eyes had learned cunning.

These things flashed through his mind without leaving an impress or meeting with question or the certainty of assent. His thoughts became impersonal, and thence he inclined to pity, to mercy, or at least the putting aside of his own quarrel with this unhappy man who obviously was speaking the truth. In hurried tones, automatically, he began reassuring him.

"No, of course, there's no use worrying about it. Carson would make the most of that." He only needed to speak to reveal the direction of his sympathy now. At once there was a brightening appreciation in Mr. Lethen's manner. "Instead, everything should be done to get at the root of the trouble. . . . Does Arvin know about it?"

"Yes, but that was in the early part. He kind of laughed when I brought it up, and said that his father had queer notions – trying to hush it up as though it didn't amount to anything. He said his father wouldn't really sue when it came to the point. I think Arvin means well. . . . But he's got into the way of giving way to everything his father says."

"Yes. No matter how absurd. And what about Carson himself? Have you actually spoken to him directly about the matter recently?"

An embarrassing hesitancy seemed to shape an answer otherwise in the same tones of melancholy. "Just half an hour ago, or less. He was in his oats field pulling mustard when I went to see whether we couldn't come to some understanding. He didn't want to listen to me at all," said the old man with a sheepish smile. "Finally, I told him I didn't think it would pay to go ahead; I guessed the world hadn't got so bad but what the public opinion would make it hot for him. Then he did get started! He said – why, he went right up in the air, and talked so fast you couldn't hear yourself think. I'd see how much people thought of me, he said. They'd forgotten I was alive, long ago. Years ago, he said, I used to strut around like a lord. We'd see the way public opinion regarded me! Why, I didn't deserve to own a farm, the way I go on. That's what makes it right for him to do me out of my property. He wouldn't let me tell him that though; he was going at such a rate that one couldn't hear himself think. The things he didn't think up weren't very many! There's no use trying to repeat them all." Mr. Lethen winced. "And perhaps he's right, and people are really indifferent. A new generation. . . . I am a back number. What he told me were private affairs which couldn't concern him at all – personal matters, you understand. Then he wound up by telling me he'd do his worst; he'd put me on the road, bag and baggage, if I tried to stop him. Unusual logic. They'd been easy with me on the mortgage, he said, and as for that it's true some of these hard years I've only been able to pay the interest. But now he wants to make that right by taking the farm away from me. He put that quite plainly, without even saying, 'If you don't pay me what you owe me.' He thinks there's no likelihood of that. He thinks I can't, and he'll just take it. Oh, I never saw such a man!"

The listener had been lost in thought while the voice went on, reaching him almost unwittingly. It was to him as if the ghost of some lost part of himself were speaking. An angleworm twisted in a shiny clod of the freshly-turned earth, its two halves separate. He looked up, as though coming to himself, but without words, and Mr. Lethen lifted his arms from the rail, as though about to turn away.

"Well, I'm sorry to have stopped you this way. If Carson notices it won't make things any better. . . . I hope you won't think I stop anybody like this and pour out a tale of woe. It seemed to me that I knew you, after knowing your people. Just the same it does a man good to talk about his troubles, you know. . . ."

"Of course," Richard Milne murmured. "It's an easy service."

"But not a small one. . . . And how have things been going with you since you left this part of the country?"

The old man obviously wanted to make conversation, as though unwillingly but inevitably impelled toward further confidences. Or perhaps to delay as long as possible going away, and abandonment to his own misgiving and despair, his solitude. He talked and made mild replies about the weather and the crops, with a look of solicitude about his dimmed green-grey eyes, his fallen face, and grey temples, stringy grey moustache. Yet it was all as though this were an old ritual with which he had many times cajoled despair, tried to warm his heart, made cold by a contact of most searching and intimate hatred. Perhaps alone with Ada Lethen he had talked thus, while she listened with a still look, gazing across the country, replying with far-off echoes of sympathy. . . . He was like a grey, unhappy, little boy, this withered man.

Richard made sympathetic interjections, and at length, without transition, he said, almost in spite of himself, "I'll see what I can do, Mr. Lethen. I'm sorry more than I can tell you to see such troubles here. I'll probably see you, or let you know what can be done. Don't worry in the meantime. Such things as he talks about don't very often really come to pass, fortunately. And I'm sure not this time if I can help it." Richard fixed his dark eyes upon the other, while his firm voice with continuity deepened, the voice of one who knew his mind, and in most cases was accustomed to acting accordingly.

The old man's eyes filled with tears. "I hope not. I'll – hope not. You don't know what it would mean. Well!" he cried desperately. "It simply can't happen, that's all. Not to me." His desperation spoke a word which his trembling lips tried to conceal. No, he would not live. Mrs. Lethen would never know before. . . . He turned away and was gone, with braced steps twisting across the clearing toward the sound of cowbells.

Richard Milne turned his team about, lowered the levers of the cultivator, and took his way back along another row of corn. The trouble, he recognized, was real enough, if only a peril in the old man's imagination. For as many years as he had dwelt in his mortifications he was inured to them, and he would not have come with this appeal to a comparative stranger unless by an actual compulsion. The security of a lifetime on one plane was upset, and, since on the side of his relation with his wife he lived in chaos, he would seem to be left with nothing to which he could hold.

Richard Milne's mood softened to pity, passed through reasoning to a hardened resolve to get at the bottom of the affair, to have it out with Carson Hymerson.

The latter had treated him lately with an insistent deference, irritating because it was dictated by the consciousness of possessing the services of a hired man without paying him wages. In spite of the contempt beneath for one so lax, this attitude was contrasted with the indifferently veiled acrimony he accorded his son. Carson's conscience, galvanized within him by thousands of such little calculations (he felt roughly like a big boy taking candy from a kid), made him muster contempt for people who would so willingly serve his needs.

The two young men were linked in this. He felt that he was over-reaching both. Milne recalled his speech to a neighbour, who complained of the flightiness of hired help. "My boys stay right by me!" Then Carson looked around to see whether Milne, splitting wood at the dooryard, had heard – almost hopefully.

Even his humour did not seem winning. One rainy day they hauled manure, burnt dry and acid-white. The load steamed rankly. "This'll loosen up your colds!" Carson's thick, short mouth had pursed.

The horses reached the rail line-fence again, the rustling through the corn ceased, and there was a cry from just before him. For a moment he could see nothing, then Ada came into view between the heads of the horses. Her face seemed blanched, with surprise reflected from his own face, he thought at first. She almost ran toward him. Haste increased her natural, long-limbed grace.

"Did you see my father?" she gasped. "Quick, tell me, did you see him?"

Dread surmise constricted him. "Why, Ada!" His voice

made it seem as though he spoke to remind both himself and her that she was that Ada Lethen of his world. But her distraught, listening face turned to him made him reply.

"Yes, your father was here not half an hour ago. Surely nothing's happened –"

"Thank God! No, perhaps not." She was turning away, as it were automatically, on the satisfactory reply to her burning anxiety, then glanced at him again. "Oh, I was afraid!"

"But, Ada! Tell me –" He had leaped from the cultivator and was leaning over the fence.

"It would take too long – too long a story, and I must go and look for him."

"He was here, and told me about it. Carson Hymerson says he is going to –"

"Put us on the road! Yes. He has been so subdued of late, and I wondered what it could be – as if he hadn't enough to bear already!" Her voice broke. "And to-day he told me, and something about the way – something in his manner – I began to think about it this afternoon, and I came out to talk it over with him. I looked all over the farm and I can't find him. You're sure then? Which way did he go?" Uncertainty gathered on her brow again.

"Quite sure. He told me all the details, and what Carson said. It seemed to relieve his mind to a certain degree. About half an hour ago he left me, right here, going into the bush again. I promised him that I would see Carson and find out what could be done. Ada! Please believe me, there's nothing happened, nothing can happen. I'll see that the business is straightened out."

"Oh, Richard! You can?" She leaned weakly against the fence. His name on her lips quickened him. "I can't seem to get over my foolish fright!" Her slender hand pressed her heart.

With a smooth movement, as though premonitory of one on his part, she had started away almost before he knew. Her swift, limber steps went over the close-bitten grassy knolls, among the ant-hills and mulleins, into the bush. He formed his lips to call her, then stopped, looking after her vanishing form, and opened his mouth again.

"Ada!" He was on the ground, beside the cultivator. "Wait!"

She turned, and he made for the fence, forgetful of the team which might run away.

"No, no!"

So fierce an impulsion of will was in her voice, in her bearing as she looked at him, that he stopped, his mind full of their last parting. As she vanished he called again.

In a fever of haste he turned to the cultivator and the team. In the middle of the field the team shied, and a figure emerged from the rustling corn, the oldest Burnstile boy, in clothes too large, his tow head bare, his small blue eyes grave. "Hello, Mr. Milne!" he cried. Milne urged the team on automatically as he returned the salutation. "I've been looking for Mr. Lethen's hat."

"Your own hat you mean, don't you, Tom?" Perhaps it had been a gift.

"No, Mr. Lethen's. You know old man Lethen, don't you? Well, I was in the bush," the boy shouted shrilly, following in the corn row, "and I seen him and old Carson over in the field. They didn't know I was seeing them, and they were going it hot and heavy. Fin'lly Hymerson up and hits old man Lethen –"

"What?"

"Hits him, knocks him for a row. Knocks his hat off. Pretty soon old man Lethen comes to his own bush where I was, and he tells me he's lost his hat coming by Carson's field, and wanted me to go look for it."

"Here," said Milne, never stopping the horses, pulling out a quarter. "Go and find the hat and take it to Mr. Lethen." He trotted the outfit into the lane, and dust rose from the wheels of the cultivator as he jogged the heavy horses.

When he reached the barn, Carson Hymerson was coming out of the stable door with a sigmoid smile on his face, which vanished to reappear almost as quickly.

"Well, you're late a little; maybe five minutes after six. Was that the reason you trotted the horses? I suppose you were trying to make up for the time you lost. I seen you talking to that old loafin' blatherskite. You'd think he'd have more shame than to lean on the fence and talk an hour, taking up people's time. If it was me –"

The man had been tying up the lines of the team while he poured out an easy stream of words. Now he came to their heads at the same time as Milne came from the other side. Richard looked at him steadily. He stopped, confused, but unable to avoid that intense gaze.

"Is what he said true?" The voice was like the blow of an axe-head.

"True," grumbled the other. "How do I know what the old blatherer's been saying?"

Lifted on a wave of fury, Richard forgot everything. He did not know the roaring sound of his own voice.

"You know very well what he was saying; you needn't look at me in that hangdog manner. I want to know! Is it true you are going to foreclose his mortgage?"

Carson shrank away. "My own's my own, and I'll do what I please with it," he mumbled.

RAYMOND KNISTER

"You'd better answer me!" Richard's voice had risen to a bellow of pure rage which no action could ever match. "Look here. You go ahead with your doings; get the sheriff out here. Put this man off his farm if you can. I want you to understand that at the first step *I'm* going to get the best lawyer money can hire, and fight it to the last. You think a lawsuit will ruin Lethen. Well, we'll see how that works on you. I'll put everything behind this thing, if necessary. My signature is good for quite as much as you can get together, understand that. Meanwhile!"

Carson threw up an arm, but too late. Richard Milne's right fist had knocked him, half-turning, to the ground six feet away.

"Little cur! . . . . Foretaste. . . ."

Richard muttered, looking at Carson's removal almost with astonishment. His arm felt foreign to him, as he strode over the plank walk to the house.

A smell of burnt pepper on the frying eggs greeted him. Lemon spots from level sunlight on the walls, as he spoke to the farmer's wife without looking at her.

"Mrs. Hymerson, I wish you would make out my bill. I won't be staying with you any further. Can you have it ready when I come down?"

Upstairs in his room he packed with collected haste, astonished afresh at the meagreness of the effects with which he had spent all this time. There was a murmur of voices outside, then a shout as the man entered and found him absent.

"I won't have the skunk in my house. You tell him his time's come, or I will. Think I'm going to have such a –" The voice went on.

Milne took three heavy steps across his floor, which was above the kitchen, and smiled at the sudden silence.

When he came down the farmer was not in the room. There were tears in Mrs. Hymerson's eyes and she could scarcely face him, but she half-heartedly insisted that he remain for the meal.

"I'm sorry that this had to happen, Mrs. Hymerson," he said finally. He unfolded a yellow bill from his small roll. "I would like to thank you for your kindness in taking me in. And I think I'd better tell you that our trouble is that Mr. Hymerson has decided to foreclose the mortgage on the Lethen place. Of course, I shall not allow that to happen. I don't say that it will not be met, but if he becomes too hasty I am sure that there will be no hesitancy in fighting the case." He turned from the kitchen door, raising his hat.

"Good-bye, Mr. Milne. You mustn't think too hardly of us on account of this."

"Indeed not. It probably will blow over. But I think that under the circumstances I'd better not stay. Good-bye."

"Good-bye."

Arvin Hymerson confronted him in the yard. For a moment the two eyed each other, Milne still holding his club-bag. The young farmer spoke non-committally.

"I ought to lick you if what my father says is true."

"Well," said Milne with a drawl and a gleam, "if that is the way you look at it, I had better tell you beforehand, while I think of it, that I have nothing against you, Arvin. Later it might slip my mind. Probably what your father told you is true as far as it goes." The other looked at him more doubtfully. "I call it mighty strange actions on the part of your father. He has been strange to all that I knew of him, ever since I came here. I can't make him out."

"Yes," spoke Arvin with sorrowful quietness. "I don't understand myself. It didn't use to be so bad. Or perhaps I notice more. . . . I think he gets more like he was as a boy, though he's not so terribly old, either. He was the youngest, and they used to pick on him, he told me. . . ."

The young man hesitated, unwilling to go on with what might appear a justification. A flash of Milne's never-remote literary interest came to the surface, to be quelled in brusqueness. He held out his hand, which the other grasped.

"I can see well enough what's the matter with him. Well-known psychological type. Good-bye."

A thrill of elation under his thoughts, Milne turned on his heel and walked down the lane to the road.

Then he recalled his parting with Ada Lethen.

TEN

A clinking of dishes and cutlery told Milne that the Burnstile family was at supper when he crossed their lawn and stepped on the veranda in the mellow, mote-filled sunlight. Bill, the father, in shirt sleeves, called over the head of the girl who had come to open the screen-door.

"Just in time. Come in." He appeared unsurprised. There were smiles on the faces of the children, as though at an old accustomed jocosity.

"Sit down. I was telling them," Bill continued, "about Devil John Jones. Do you mind him? He used to be around – perhaps you wouldn't see so much of him as us older fellows. Anyway, one day he came to Dad and wanted to sell him a pig. Well, the pig looked kind of runty, and my father wasn't particular about it, but he agreed to keep it a few days anyway, since Devil John was bound to unload the brute right there and then. You see, if he didn't buy, and sent it back, old John would be ahead that much feed." Here Johnnie choked with laughter, and, glancing at him with enjoyment, Bill continued the drawling narrative.

"Well, they puts Mr. Pig into a pen alone, and Dad feeds him right away, puts a big tubful of swill into the trough in front of him. Old John stayed around quite a while, chewing the fat and dickering for some other head of stock, and then they went back after a while and took another look at the pig again. Every bit of that swill was gone. Pig had ate it all. Well, Dad ups and reaches into the pen, takes that pig by the ears and tail, and hoists him out of the pen and into the tub that had held the swill. And that doggone pig wouldn't fill that tub! Well, sir, that was enough for my father. He said he didn't want anything more to do with an animal like that, that ate more than his own size in one meal. Had your supper, Richard?"

"Well, no –"

Milne's voice held a reserve scarcely adjusted to the scene before him. In this there was a comforting familiarity which seemed to delete the emotions of the past days and at once to bring into focus a homely reality.

"Sit in here then."

Mrs. Burnstile, whom he had met but once, seconded the invitation, as she rose and brought extra dishes to the table. Part of the children got up and circulated about the room, while some of them remained seated. He was served with soft, warm fried potatoes and cold ham, tea, and apple sauce and cake.

After supper Richard accompanied Bill to his chores at the barn. His suitcase on the veranda reminded him of the need of explanation, and he asked whether he might spend a few weeks there. He had a sense that the other regarded this as almost unnecessary form, so casually had he been received; and he felt so fully that he had been there a long time that it seemed superfluous to mention an indefinite stay.

Bill nodded. "Fall out with Carson? I kind of thought it would come. If you think you can enjoy your vacation here amongst my tribe, you're perfectly welcome."

Richard explained that he might like occasionally to take some exercise in the fields, if he could be of use, but that he didn't want any dependence to be placed upon his availability. In fact, as though he had held a thankless, altruistic purpose of service to Carson Hymerson, he was inclined to repudiate such an intention altogether now. He felt the need of asserting independence. He would pay his way and maintain strictly the aloofness of a summer boarder. But if people showed themselves congenial he was prepared to be accommodating. This feeling probably arose from his sense of some appearance of the ridiculous in his obstinacy, his sticking to this countryside, after Ada Lethen had attempted definitely to break with him, and he had been unable to get on with his host.

In truth he was more or less dazed, and the celerity and ease with which upsetting things happened seemed prophetic of still more catastrophic events in the future. He had a sense of fatality and sometimes his conjectures regarding the outcome made him determine that his resolve, or his tendency, to proceed slowly was justified. It had required only the events of the last few days to make him doubt his position and, almost, his feelings. Ada Lethen – was it in her or his engrossed dream that she had appeared to him that afternoon?

Bill agreed briefly to his proposal. Would his wife favour it? Richard solved the problem by his bearing, his interest in the children, and consciously by proffering to Mrs. Burnstile the amount of two weeks' board in advance.

Long before those days had passed he felt that he knew the healing of change and time in that gregarious family, and the partaken freedom of young growing things about him. He was diverted, even absorbed, by the ceaseless interplay and careless activity of the children; and before long he was part of it, in the confidence the boys and girls had for him.

The kids would bother him, Bill Burnstile had prophesied, and there was not long a doubt of this, with the insistence of the boys in escorting nearly all of his daytime walks. While his mind bent over pondered thoughts his eyes would follow their antics, or he would return wholly to listen to their absurd talk.

They seemed almost to have accepted as a duty the part of entertainers, and wrestled, chased, and bantered each other remorselessly and without weariness. They were rewarded for hours if Richard Milne burst into an involuntary laugh when Bill and Tom wrestled themselves into weird shapes, or, becoming angry, fought with clods of earth from behind trees until they laughed at themselves. And they had always a marvellous tale of their immediate experience they must share.

"Mr. Milne," the vivacious red Bill chattered. "Mr. Milne, you know that rat I had?" Richard recalled a mouse they had caught in a screen trap, nearly dead, with a hole in its side.

"Mine, it was," claimed the older Tom, looking up from his feet, which were pawing the soft turf. Johnnie, his soft, dark eyes gleaming, looked shyly with understanding from them to the man. Bill's tones rose.

"Yours it was not! Well, I had it. You know? I killed him and he jumped away."

"And how did you kill him?" Richard asked.

"Jumped on him, of course. Both heels." When Bill demonstrated, Johnnie squealed, jumping likewise. "And he jumped." Bill adapted a wiggling motion of the hand to the word. "And jumped! And I killed him and he jumped!"

Slow-witted Tom wanted to know, literally, though he had been present at the execution, how the rat could jump after he had been killed.

"Easy."

"Yeah, I bet you couldn't if you was killed."

"Oh, yes, I could. I'd jump around like a chicken without a head."

Though the others got into most of the mischief, Johnnie seemed to enjoy the greatest zest in it, adding that of the spectator to the part he played. Their fights were transitory, fierce, and soon forgotten, but Bill was usually the aggressor. His older brother was half-afraid of him; but Johnnie, when once in a while he was fully roused, could take his own part with him or the growthy, open-mouthed Tom.

The practically complete irresponsibility of their life was like a fresh revelation to Milne, who enjoyed it for them more fully than they did. Their father seemed to allow them all freedom, but the truth was that he forgot them until some of the stock broke out and had to be herded in by "all hands," or some chore had to be left to them when he went with his team to the field. They were impelled by projects and curiosity embracing the whole extent of farm routine and phenomena. They could find amusement in tumbling down a strawstack, hissing the gander, clinging to the tail of a gambolling calf, building what they called a "suspension bridge" over a ditch by means of ropes, dog-chains, and the stakes from a corn-planter. Or they were diverted by merely wandering about the fields and lanes.

The weather became rainy, but they were not deterred. They liked to find places, such as the road or the lane, where the fine, paste-like mud would squelch through their toes; and, bursting into shouts, they commenced a race "on a heavy track," as Bill explained, while they slipped, fell, and rose with a mass of mud smeared over their clothes.

Their mother was a red-headed, blue-eyed Scotch woman of rapid tongue and a mind of her own, which she exercised but little except when her inclinations were crossed. Bill Burnstile had run across her in the West, and, since she seemed a capable sort of woman for a housekeeper, and a good sport, he had married her. He had liked her smartness, but now she appeared to have become somewhat lackadaisical in her attitude toward life. She paid perfunctory attention to the children, and, beyond a casual word now and then to the effect that they were not to "bother Mr. Milne," she betrayed little interest in preventing them from conducting themselves as they pleased.

This easy-going character showed itself in her housework as well, and if she had been inclined toward rationalization, she might have held that it manifested part of her equipment for self-preservation. For if she had tried alone to take care of the house and every need of her family, she would have been run to death. And rest was one of the things to which she was normally inclined. She was healthy, usually content, and so were the children, with access to the pantry whenever they cared for "a piece," and without inhibitions regarding manners or the care of furnishing or their clothes.

She customarily took the mornings for cooking, churning, or sweeping, care of the poultry; some afternoons for mending, and much time for an incidental and almost unconscious idleness, in which she read magazines, arranged her hair, or talked to her girls, to the neighbours by telephone, or slept.

The girls themselves were three – Alice, wistful, nervous, emphatic, fifteen, who was to start to high school in the coming autumn; Ellen, thirteen and older than any of the boys, a thin, pale, little thing with blue eyes, gentle voice, and a determined mouth; and Mary, younger than Johnnie, with deep gold hair uncommon for a child so young, blue-grey eyes, merry lips never still and usually moistened with fruit.

Richard Milne spent much of his day in wandering about the country, chatting over fences with old neighbours and new, drinking in impressions of the life he had known, or making a vague effort to impose exterior circumstances upon his attention, to let them supersede his inner conflict. But mostly he was unable to decide why he should make an effort toward anything. At first he had thought of going directly, not to Ada Lethen, but to her parents. Perhaps they could come to an understanding which would alter the whole situation. They did not realize, surely, what they were doing to Ada Lethen, what they had done. If they retained any natural affection they could be made to see. If they did not . . . He pictured himself standing between the ageing man and woman, impelling them to speak, to know each other. . . . But he could not decide whether this was a wise thing to do, and, particularly because he desired to make a scene of that sort on account of the acrimony engendered in him during the last few weeks, he was reluctant to trust himself in such a situation. Or if he could trust himself, he could not trust unforeseeable factors in the predicament. Did he not have good reason? He could not know what Ada Lethen would do, in any case.

Yet, as he had always told himself, she had common sense; she had restraint, or she should not have been where she was for the reasons for which she was there. He had told himself as an uncompromising realist that she had, she must possess, faults. Yet he could not label them. He saw excuses, reasons for the delinquencies, failings which annoyed him most, and these reasons in the sadness of her life brought him back to the important, the moving, the all-important fact which animated his whole interest: he loved her. If he had not, or loved her less, anything might have been possible, everything might have been risked.

A distrust of obvious and melodramatic courses had returned upon him, so that he marvelled at what he had already done. He had promised her father his help in a lawsuit, if it should transpire that such help was needed. He had knocked Carson Hymerson down, on the other hand, and ran the risk of being hauled before the local magistrate on the charge of assault. He should have been prepared for any developments, and should have been ready, now that the ice was broken, to adopt a course of action that would get him what he wanted. Yet he was held back. If he sought the Lethens out, with his present feelings to all three, he would probably secure the enmity of two at least, and Ada one of them. No, he would wait until he saw clearly his course.

He was capable of that, though at moments the country was a prison cell up and down which he walked. He would wait, and if nothing came of the difficulty with Hymerson, the way would seem clearer, or at least no less simple, if that were an advantage, than it had always been. If the dispute came to actual court proceedings, the matter would be complicated infinitely, and perhaps against his will he would be forced into a part which would win, and certainly would earn, the favour of the Lethens. What a subject it would be for local talk!

Again, if the case were lost and they were put off the farm, Ada would refuse to leave the old people, and her gratitude would be no more than an embarrassing burden. He shuddered. Won, still more embarrassing would be the regard of the parents, if they showed any – fortified, not shaken from their old positions. They might even recognize his right to marry Ada, give their consent, and he might find himself bound to continue assistance, remaining with Ada in this place. His old resentment against the unhappy couple returned, mingled with a perverse pride. He would not flatter them with his help; he would conquer them without their knowing it. And he would prefer that their true colours should be revealed to Ada – if she could recognize them. With all his dislike for both Mr. and Mrs. Lethen, which blurred their images directly they were removed from his presence, he could not quite assure himself that they would show just the degree of obtuse acrimony, the stupid resentment, which might be calculated to make Ada see them as they appeared to himself.

Meanwhile he was wise to stay away, in a life of the casual summer-holiday boarding type which he had always scorned. Carson, he knew, believed his threat of taking part in any proceedings, and if he did assume bravado enough to begin, could soon be brought to time. And Mr. Lethen would still not be tempted to venture into hostilities needlessly, as he might had Richard continued to reassure him. But his story might not have contained the whole truth. Perhaps, Milne's more detached judgement told him, it would prove to be six of one and half a dozen of the other, so that right and wrong would prove indistinguishable, in the commonly wearisome and costly manner.

Divided in mind, even whilst almost obsessed, Richard found no respite. At times he was disgusted with himself. What should he have to do with such people? It seemed to him at times that he had placed himself at the mercy of the unrea- son of two probably inexcusable and needlessly contentious peasants. Of course, he was not compelled to have anything to do with them. No matter what happened, he could refuse to stir, and even Ada scarcely could blame him.

But he knew only too well that he would feel obliged to redeem his words, or at least do his best to discover where the rights or wrongs of the matter lay. For once having begun any enterprise, he was fatally constituted to follow it through to finality. Otherwise he should have been far away at that moment.

Richard Milne's dissatisfaction had spread to include all things without and within him; no longer was he simply rankling with the irony of the thwarted male. Every move he made drew him further into an irrelevant maze. He wondered whether it would not be just as wise to resort to extreme measures – elope with Ada Lethen, carry her off if necessary, or take himself away for ever. Yet, as he kept telling himself, he had only to think of the woman herself to know the futility of any course which might occur to him. It seemed that the perfections with which she had been endowed in his mind made part of her inaccessibility, so that he could not "think success," in the locution of inspired commerce.

Yet it would have been the logical outcome of his earlier mood, intensified by its own momentum, or aggravated by any mere catastrophe, to take drastic measures. The night of that very day he had come to conclusions with Carson he had felt with elation that anything was possible. But that was past. He could do nothing, really, not even think effectually – but wait, and that not patiently. He was inclined to blame his own mind and hers, intricate mechanisms constructed for purposes futile, pathetically ridiculous and grandiose.

ELEVEN

The bewitched summer was passing, to the senses imperceptibly, and generally to his dissatisfaction. It seemed to typify that rural dilatoriness which doubtless kept Carson Hymerson from taking the steps he had threatened in his lawsuit with Lethen; and it gave no hope of coming certainty, no illusion of progression or rumour of hope.

In the morning Richard Milne, after breakfast with the family and automatically meticulous care in grooming, walked alone to the front gate, along the road to the big gate before the barn on the edge of the ridge; he looked at the stock in the yard, perhaps fastened one end of the neck yoke when Bill Burnstile was hitching his team for the morning's work in the field. The young man surveyed the crops, variegated squares, from the slope, and descended into the orchard back of the house before completion of what the children called going "round the block," and returned to the veranda.

There were green small winter apples in the orchard, and harvest apples already becoming yellow. There were spots of deep shade. He always expected his reveries to be broken

into by sight or sound of one or more of the children hiding
behind the reddish trunks, which had been rubbed smooth
by the grazing animals. Any of them might be lurking in
the higher grass or in the thick, poorly-pruned limbs of the
trees themselves. Little Mary seemed to haunt the place, not
regarding the presence or absence of the others; and the
child's capabilities in climbing and hiding were part of an
abiding mystery. Richard offered to lift her down from a
bough above seven feet of smooth trunk, but she laughed and
went on with her talking. She talked apparently as much for
herself as for any hearer. It was not the usual child's fairy
stories, concerned with princes, angels, dollies, and posies, but
as he heard her breathless voice in the distance, "an' . . . an'
. . . an' . . .", he knew that she was embroidering some stupid
literal circumstance or object in her little world.

Passing that way again, tired of himself and the idle
depression of his mind, the man would stop and listen.

"Johnnie, he went way up *in* the tree and lookeded in
the robins' nest, an' robin pecked 'is hand, an' 'e comed down
quick, an' – Mr. Milne, Mr. Milne!"

"Yes."

"You know your apple tree, under your window, and
you know our cat! You know your apple tree and you know
our cat!"

"Yes, yes!"

"Well, our cat climbed right up in your apple tree." Her
gold hair gleaming in the spots of sunlight, her ruddy face
aglow, she laughed.

"Richard! Richard! One old hen, she died, and Billy –
Billy took her babies. Billy looks after them now." She laughed.
"If Ada Lethen had apples on her trees, and the robins and the
crows pecked them off, I'd be glad! If they fell on the ground

Aw'd be glad! Aw'd be glad!" Without animus she laughed at her own irresistible humour, repeating her saying, concluding with an effect of rhetoric and almost evangelical beatification, "Aw'd be glad!" She laughed with an Oriental, steady uprightness of countenance.

"There was a man here, and another man, and Johnnie liked the other man, and the other man gave him a nickel, and – Do you know what I say and Ellen says when Mamma gives us supper? Fankoo. Fankoo, we says."

Mary interrupted herself to search her mind for something more marvellous to add. "Did any of the trees in this orchard blow down in the storm? Yes, they did. Look over there at that limb blown down right to the ground."

Stormy weather made no difference apparently to the children, who might be found in the orchard, playing in the barn, or anywhere but in the house. Sometimes, at meals or when otherwise they came under the eye of their father, he ordered them to keep in out of the rain.

There were many such days. The woods and fields became soggy and wet, the long-desired rains of spring belatedly arrived to confound summer prospects. In spite of this Richard Milne had given up taking his walk along the clean, gravelled highway, in a vain determination to avoid even physical approach to the Lethens.

The days were warm, even during the heaviest rains, the sun bright and ardent immediately after. Too bright, too warm, Bill Burnstile claimed, after the first showers. The ground would cake in the dry time to follow. But it was rain and again more rain that followed. The farmers, after short space of sun in the late afternoon, went to bed certain that another day would let them on the land, which sorely needed cultivating among the matted weeds of the corn and rank tobacco; the wheat must be cut, rain or no rain, since it would certainly be lost if it were left.

And through the night of their heavy slumbers the rain would fall, softly at first upon the low roofs, then steadily half the night, in the serene and fragrant dark, with little breezes, and the earth would drink surely to satiety. In the morning the soil would appear as it had the morning previous, but it would take two more days to dry, if another shower did not follow. . . . Meanwhile the crops were being smothered with weeds, the grain was beaten to the ground, in some cases left until over-ripe and then lodged and shelled by storm.

Something in this rhythmic replenishing of the fecund and steaming earth calmed Richard Milne without quite pleasing him, as he walked about the black ground of the hollows, the lighter gravel land of the tobacco ridges. Along the river there were many gullies and ditches overgrown, in which the rank vegetation smothered the raw outlines of the ground. In a swamp a forest, a pond of nettles higher than a man's head waved acridly, wavered and bowed like long trees, fern-like, in the light breeze, some recoiling more quickly than others, jostling and bowing back and forth to each other. They had a symbolic malevolence, a blue-green sea of fire, and Richard Milne watched it for moments without thinking.

Sumach grew densely along moist ditches, rank, with stalks as thick as a man's arm, little groves towering branchless twenty feet, at that height to spread a thick thatch of green which withstood light showers: it was like tropical vegetation. That year the elderberries grew thick and weighty on brittle stalks, changing from discs of cream frothiness to dark, pendulous spheres of fruit, purple, which almost seemed to swell with the increasing rains.

The richness of greenery and bitter yellow, blue-grey stems, purple fruit, stretched above his head, seeming to bury his consciousness as he walked about the overgrown ravines, the knolls, and hollow places. The man would stop and sit on a bank under the canopy of sumach and stare at the ground, black earth strewn with rusty stems of the sumach leaves of other years, thinking of those times and of Ada Lethen, while the rain began to patter unheeded above him. So long he had been forced into a rôle of waiting that he scarcely could believe in the singleness of his intention to escape. Did he really want her as he had been telling himself so long? Was his desire sincere? How could he know? In all else his decision, his will sufficed. In this course he showed himself a veritable Hamlet. But the mere thought of all their difficulties seemed to paralyse his faculties. Surely it was some bewitched aura of that ill-starred older pair. Perhaps, if he should take Ada Lethen, happiness would never result. It might be a violation of the natural course which would wrench them away from all seemly conduct of life and fill their lives with disaster.

"All their difficulties." It appeared to him that they were joined in struggle with those at least, though what joined them were the instrument of their separation. As with ill-starred lovers of romance, Tristram and Iseult, Lancelot and Guinevere, the craven bully Fate seemed to have taken a spite against them, and would never remit his rancour. He saw this aspect seldom, and indeed it might have been his acceptance of it as a commonplace which determined his bent toward romance in his creative efforts, while it made him credit literally the prohibition which walled in Ada Lethen.

But besides this he could not forget all his failures. She was so identified with them, he saw, that it was a wonder that his love could endure. Yet it did, and though at moments of desperation he was almost decided to risk any action, resolve was neutralized by the annoyance attending memory of small past absurdities, the memory which leaves a greater sting than that of our disasters and our mistakes. . . . So it was that he had become one with a sense of frustration and releasing melancholy which permitted him to see all things as though they were portions of a futilely past dream.

The clouds thickened. Nothing, he was sure, could hurt him more than he had been hurt; he had nothing to fear unless, at worst, returning to this city, that old hunger would envelop him, twisting him to its shapes before he could bury himself in work. There, where, his mind told him, he could see that face behind all his trouble, he would be almost at peace after a time in a struggle perpetual, and perpetually baffled even by success. Only, in the parks, theatres, on the streets, in photographs even, there would be couples, beautifully oblivious. . . . Ah! Their smiles, trusting eyes. Happy! He smiled grimly. Perhaps he was not a happy man; too determined. Nor was he, evidently, determined enough. What determined men did, he did not know. They did not abduct recalcitrant ladies, certainly, as he was thinking of doing. Presumably they forgot, in a sea containing better fish than ever had come out of it.

He had stopped, bemused, and he now saw that he was not alone. A short, drab-clothed figure was standing near by, looking at him fixedly through the half-mist of the dull afternoon. Richard wondered how long this person had been standing there watching him, before he recognized the bumpy, hard features of Carson Hymerson under the slouched brim of his old hat. There was nothing menacing in his attitude. Rather it was as though he were trying to decide whether

Richard would permit him to approach and greet him after what had passed between them.

Richard started to move away, but Carson was approaching him with a sheepish grin.

"Funny little weather, ain't it?" he remarked, as though they had parted an hour ago. "Great day for – for ducks."

Richard remained silent, but he nodded non-committally, wondering what was on the other's mind.

"Funny way of farming, the old bird has," Carson continued, looking about at the underbrush and the weeds and nettles in the bog before him. "The place sure needs somebody to take hold and take an interest in it. Of course, there is some waste land on it, bound to be, where that peat bog was burnt over. But when I've had it a couple of years and get it ploughed under, you won't know the farm. You want to come back some time and see it, Richard. Always welcome, you know. No hard feelings." He spoke in a tone of magnanimity, yet as though expecting that his good intentions would not be credited.

Richard had an impulse to laugh. He looked at the man steadily. "So you intend to go ahead and try to put this man off his property?"

"Well, it sounds like it, don't it?" Carson laughed. "I – we all want what's ours, don't we?"

"Yes," agreed Milne drily, "but we have different ideas about what is ours."

"That doesn't matter," said Carson. "That won't hinder me any."

The doggedness of his tone aroused a perverse streak in Milne. He would ignore the whole matter.

"How are Mrs. Hymerson and Arvin keeping?" he inquired blandly, as though he had heard nothing.

"All right," growled Carson. "Old Lethen may think I'm going to let him off, but I ain't. Not any more. I'm out to get what's mine, and don't you forget to tell him."

"This weather is not the most favourable for the crops, is it? How is that piece of corn doing which I was cultivating? It must be getting rather weedy, is it not?"

"They been a public nuisance long enough, the Lethens. It's time somebody got stirred up about them."

A flush came into Richard's cheeks, but he continued calmly.

"The quarrels and bickerings of children are very amusing, are they not? I find it so, for example, in the case of Bill Burnstile's family. I have been stopping with them. I suppose you knew."

Carson looked as though words would be inadequate to express his infuriation.

"You tell him from me to go to hell. I don't care for him and all his friends with him," he yelled, stamping his feet.

Richard looked at him in some surprise. This was not the tone of the crafty mortgage holder, nor yet of Carson as he knew him. He shrugged his shoulders and turned away.

"Tell them all to go to hell!" Carson yelled again.

It occurred to Richard that he might inform the man that he was trespassing on the property of others, but he was doing the same thing himself. . . . In the same bland tone he called back:

"Let us hope that there'll be fair weather for a few days anyway." He chuckled as he turned away.

Unheeding the rain, which was slackening, he pursued his way to the Burnstile house, there to find a flare of early lamplight brightening the steam from cookery in the warm kitchen – which was filled with the swarming children. Bill the older came in with full milk pails; he had done most of the chores before the late supper. Nothing could dull the interest of these elusively vital children, with their preoccupations of mischief and pique and jollity. And after bantering them, listening to some drawled story of Burnstile's experience in the West, to which his wife at the other end of the table gave a lazily enigmatic smile, he went to his room and lit a lamp.

There, after looking through a haphazard pile of popular magazines, he took up *The Scarlet Letter*, one of the three books, along with Bunin's stories and *Wilhelm Meister's Wanderjahre*, which he had brought with him. In a short time he blew the light out and settled for the night.

But he could not sleep. Phrases and images from *The Scarlet Letter* floated in his mind. He was expiating Dimmesdale's secret sin yet, after two centuries. Love could not be free yet for men and women who had taken civilization as an armour which had changed to fetters upon them. What was his whole piacular story but that of Dimmesdale – prophetic name – a delusion no longer a delusion of sin, but of impotence and analysis which belied action and love? It was the conflict of the conscious ones of his whole generation, this confusion of outer freedom and inner doubt.

He could not sleep, and for the first and the last time he was visited by the desire to rise and walk in the night. He derided the notion for a time, and then asked, "Why not?" He went down through the intimately silent house, which he could not believe held those exuberant children, into the moon-held yard, into a baffled certainty that there could be no certainty. For a lover's premonition, untrustworthy as them all, led him to feel that Ada Lethen was walking that road, and he would meet her. . . . There were only the clouds, smoky-blue over the phosphorescent moon, with a sort of feinting mockery which veiled suggestive things, only a minute later to reveal their commonplace nonentity.

He stopped before the gloom of the Lethen house, peered among its black shadows, looked to the dulled windows, the vines which were now and again carved into relief by the moonlight, and, instead of turning back, he walked past. But it was equally vain, and, coming back, he hurried past the place as though a ghost dwelt there; and, he knew not how, came to his home and slept, not knowing in sleep that there was such a thing in the world as love, as baffled fidelity, as unrelenting aspiration. And the rain beating upon the roof above him accompanied for a time his slumber.

TWELVE

I n the morning Bill Burnstile said, "Well, I kind of didn't want to be too sure about giving up hope, but she sure does look juberous. Rains the minute you turn your back. That your doings, Richard?"

The two met in the cool morning sunlight outside the back door. Bill was coming in from the before-breakfast chores, and Richard stood on the stoop, shaven, and dressed in a grey suit and soft linen, inhaling the unflawed air.

"This'll keep you off that oats field two more days, I suppose," he agreed.

As the weeks had passed the wheat had been cut and shocked as best it might be, and for the greater part stood out through the rains, turned over with forks after each of them, in view of a day of vantage when it could be hauled into the barns or threshed in the open. The fields of standing oats were creamy ponds, awaiting the binder, but the ground was so soft that the horses could scarcely be expected to pull it.

"Looks as though it'll be September before we get around to cutting the oats, all right – if any'd be left in the heads! But I'm going to tackle that late piece that's not quite ripe first, as soon as I can get on it at all. It won't be lodged so much, being short, and besides if it is a little green, it doesn't hurt oats, that part. Ripen afterward, and like as not turn out better than the good oats this year. . . ."

"I tell you," proposed Richard, "I'll give you a hand shocking if it looks like rain." A sympathetic impatience with the weather made him anxious to see things accomplished when the opportunity did occur.

"Great!" acceded Burnstile gladly. "We'll make things hum. I was trying to round up a man or two down to the village last night. They got lots of time to talk, but none to work, unless they happen to feel like it. They're rich as long as they got a dollar. Jess Trimble says why don't I hire you. You had nothing to do but hang around that Lethen girl, what never was any good, but to keep her head stuck in books and get it crammed full of trash." He laughed.

Richard flushed, but curbed his temper. He knew that Bill had not the slightest malice in repeating such a thing, that he quoted it solely to exemplify the amusing obtuseness of local character. It had not occurred to Richard that these people had their attitude toward such anomalies as Ada Lethen and himself, and that they would be talking to no uncertain purpose. What they thought or said could be of no conceivable importance, he argued, but the gossip which Bill had repeated rankled within him.

In his writing, Richard Milne had concerned himself with such people as these, typical farm characters. But while he had blinked none of their littlenesses, critics had claimed that his novels presented too roseate a picture of rural life. The reason was that he had seemed to find these temporal idiosyncrasies set off in due proportion against the elemental materials of life. But, he reflected now, that attitude was part of the nostalgia he experienced from his own past in such scenes; and it was a form of idealism which he saw as applicable no more to this milieu than to any province of life more or less open to primal forces. He would not have idealized these in a setting of commerce or of society, and he had been wrong to blur them in a scene which his boyhood had known. Hence, he foresaw, a further development in his own art. An increasing surface hardness seemed to be an inevitable accompaniment to the progress of the significant novelists of his and an earlier day. It was curious to find himself, with his infinite sensitiveness to change in his outlook and his inner feelings, developing his relation to his work even when his whole being and all his faculties seemed to be concentrated on the image of the woman he loved.

It was, he remembered, only an image upon which all his thoughts were converged. Allowing for the beginning and the course, attended by absence and memory, of his love, he could not hope to see the woman as others saw her. It had been one of the twin deities of his life. His urge to expression – and this. Perhaps she was at the bottom of his urge to write. Otherwise she might not have remained beside all his efforts as they proceeded. And if she had been more than an ideal – or less – he should have forgotten her in turning to any one of the numbers of girls and women he had known, charming or admirable. But he had remembered her, and perhaps the function of his repeated returns was to renew the impression which her physical presence made upon him, or to free him from it. And once back in this place, so near to her, if farther than ever in spirit, he was obsessed, he could not escape her appeal to the senses. It was the more confusing after his long freedom from such feelings. He saw her face in its sad meditation, and in its proud contours. He saw the soft, even curve

of her lips, which were a continual marvel to him whenever
she came before his sight. How a girl could go through all the
spirit-chapping experiences she had known without some
weakness, some bitterness, showing in that most sensitive
feature, her mouth, was beyond his comprehension. It was not
a strong mouth, the mouth, "denoting character," which
exhibits an impervious attitude built up to withstand the
world, or an aggressive one to battle with it. Her lips showed
nothing of submission or revolt, nothing of joy or despair, in
repose, nothing but a sweet calm and an understanding sympathy not to be betrayed into sentimental sorrow, a calm
sweetness never to be betrayed into hasty greed of sensation.
Her mouth, he thought, was Ada Lethen.

Her hands, too, pale, large, narrow, graceful, and yet
easily forgotten. Her arms were slightly too slender for them,
despite her vigorous life. Her figure was slight, yet not without
modelling. Her hair was heavy and dark as night, her com-
monest gesture a turning of it aside from her forehead. She
had recently had it bobbed, though he had not noticed this
until the second meeting, in daylight, when she had sent him
away from her.

But her distinguishing mark, to a stranger, was a mole
below her left cheek, at the corner of an equilateral triangle
formed between it, her eye, and the corner of her mouth. It
was thus in the least conspicuous and yet most effective spot.
For it gave piquancy to her face, added to her otherwise
sombre beauty; made it distinguished and unforgettable,
while one would not remember explicitly, "She had a mole."
It was ornament and relief. It was the most endearing feature
in her face; its loss would have detracted greatly, and yet he
forgot constantly that she possessed it.

She came before him, night after night, and scarcely left

his daytime thoughts, more seductive than she ever was in reality. She did not in fact present such a quality to the world. He seriously doubted whether she would charm many men, even men of more than average insight. She was like some rare work of art, inordinately admired, even idolized, by a few devotees, tolerantly assessed by snobs and cognoscenti, and neglected by the world. He at least knew her value; and to him she was far more seductive even of face and limb than any woman he had encountered. Her spell was such that it met him at every point, in his memory.

Such considerations could not always be pleasant, and he was glad of any opportunity of distraction. When the following morning was again bright, Richard put on old clothes. After breakfast he and Bill got the binder out of the shed, tightened the canvases which had been unbuckled to allow for stretching from moisture, and drove back the muddy lane.

"We'll get a start anyway. The horses should hold out to get around once, wet or no wet, and it may get drier as we go."

"If it doesn't rain we'll have a dry time," Richard assented with a shout, striding behind the jingling and jolting binder, with risen spirits.

It was a day enchanted, aside from the unpleasantness under foot, with the harmonious concord usually imparted only to art or dreams. The woods held aloof in misty solitude, like a vision, though the warm air gave most objects an appearance of being near. Later, vast cool clouds began a sultry procession above the land. They hung like vast bags, bunches of dirty blue silk protruding from the meshes of a net formed by their fissures. And toward noon the sun gave them a silver radiance, hardening to metal likewise the verdigris of forests. The air was still heavy, close. Horses and men sweated copiously.

As before in the wheat-cutting, the three sizeable Percherons could pull the binder only a few rods without weakening; and when the ponderous machine slowed, the broad drive wheel slid in the soft black soil, digging furrows a foot wide, almost that deep, and as many feet long as the horses could drag the binder thus, while the heads were torn from the stalks. Soon the field was spotted with these dark trenches, as though some preternaturally active rodent had been digging his home there in great numbers. And the horses were losing their freshness, even their willingness, as though they did not expect that their best efforts would cause the binder to run more than a few yards.

Richard with a fork pitched briskly out to the fence the sheaves thrown in from the first round, so that the binder could turn and begin cutting in the normal fashion, with a leftward circuit. After that he had little to do, since several rounds had to be reaped before he could shock the bundles conveniently without carrying them too far. The sheaf-carrier, controlled by Bill Burnstile's foot, dropped the sheaves in bunches of two and three and four, at intervals the same for every round. Richard lay on a couple of sheaves and looked up to the sky. Tom, now that he was not needed to "throw out," appeared and knelt on another sheaf beside him.

"Kind of thistley, ain't it, for shocking," mentioned the boy, selecting a stalk from his sheaf, and slowly spitting through it.

Richard smiled. "Good boy! You knew that without taking hold of a single bundle, didn't you." He looked away with absent enjoyment over the country. One elm, even in the noonday light, standing against the sky on the river bank alone seemed to gather about itself a slight haze, a softness over its green.

Tom's lips twisted naïvely. "I got hold of a bundle all right, didn't I? This one I'm sitting on! . . . That's why I didn't want to shock none. Thistles are too much of a good thing, I can tell you."

Milne began to lecture lazily in a rôle of practicality. "You should have spudded the thistles out when you saw they were going to grow faster than the oats. Before they get ripe, that's the time to catch thistles. . . . Now look at that white thistledown. . . ." He puffed at his pipe dreamily. "Very pretty no doubt . . . floating over the field. . . ."

"Don't catch thistles at all, that's me, boy! Too sharp. Not in my bare feet, anyhow. When Dad got me in here to spud out the docks, I found out! There weren't many docks, though." The boy looked at his brown and mud-caked feet stuck out before him.

"Probably not many more than there are now," reflected Milne silently, looking over the field where an occasional maroon-coloured spire showed itself. The farm had been neglected in the matter of weeds before Bill Burnstile settled upon it.

Suddenly there was a scream from Tom, and, turning, Richard saw the boy's neck encircled by smaller hands. Bill and Johnnie were upon him, gasping.

"Well, are you going to slap my face?" Bill asked his older brother vindictively.

"I never said I'd slap your face. Go 'way, can't you!" Tom thrust at them, cunningly taking an injured tone as though interrupted in a grown-up colloquy. The smaller two backed away, looking at the man with laughing respect. But Tom was leaving nothing to afterclaps, and knelt on the sheaves.

"Can you do this?" he asked, attempting to stand on his hands, and falling over backward in the stubble.

Richard, for whom the display was given as much as for the marauders, glanced back as he walked away to recommence shocking, and smiled at the failure. Bill and Johnnie, witnessing this reception of the attempted feat, began to pummel Tom again, and his yells resounded in the field, uplifted in the uncertain, husky, or shrill tones of his age.

But little Johnnie came presently trotting after Richard, and watched the man work, in silence or saying words softly to himself, and occasionally running to take up an odd bundle left over, to drag it to a site where Richard could use it to build the next shock, two and two.

By noon the sunlight was clear and hot, the air still rather heavy. They had not made much impression on the field of oats. The area cut around the edge did not appear very wide. But all hands were hungry, including the boys, who rode up the lane on the three sweating horses. The perfect purity of the air was tinged by the heavy, moist smell of the grass and trees, by the animal odours of the barnyard, and finally by bacon and boiled potatoes, rhubarb pie.

After dinner the day became overcast, and Burnstile, as the two men fastened the weighty ends of the binder neck-yoke to the horses' necks, opined with a curious and unusual depression that he might as well not go on cutting; it was going to rain, sure as anything. Besides, packing the land would do it no good. He had brought Tom to the field to help, but presently the boy lingered behind Richard shocking, and slipped away into the woods beside the field, or into the lane which led to the house and barn.

Already proceeding toward the west, the sun might have been forgotten save for a cliff of cloud the shape of the map of Denmark, the illuminated top of which covered the sun, while the lower part as boundaried by a quicksilver edge. The binder was driven on doggedly, and Burnstile's shouts could be heard resounding dully from one end of the field to the other. The hair of the horses was roughened and spiked with sweat, and when they stopped at one corner of the uncut rectangle, where Richard was working, Bill could be heard, apparently talking half to himself:

"I don't know what's got into me, seem so stupid to-day. Horses, if you have your off days when you don't feel any funnier than I do just now, and you've got to work, I feel sorry for you."

Richard smiled absently as one who listens to a child, and gathered two more bundles in his abraded hands. The strip which had been cut around the field was dark with the stubble of rank weeds and the black soil. There was a rhythmic swish as he strode on, stooping to catch up one bundle and then another to put under the other arm. The sharp, crisp rectangle of uncut oats in the centre of the field was cream-tipped, stretching away out of sight, and the pale blue bottoms of the stalks gleamed in a strange light.

Wind arose, and blew the thistledown about the oats field, to the imperturbable bush, like swarms of some swift insect bent on a common goal; and a few like bubbles settled in the black trenches dug by the starting binder. Day was overcast, and it seemed that the elements were bent on a dreadful play before some outburst of passion. Swallows high in the air seemed higher against the dark smoke-blue of a storm cloud, ecstatically battling with the wind, hanging stationary and struggling against it, while one lone bird executed a long, straight dart of half a mile at aeroplane speed with the gale.

The oats field and the gloomy light were curiously lethargic in their tranquillity, even the forests seemed to toss with a heavy, slow resignation which was strange to the tumult above the earth. At the south-west, above the horizon, glowed light, cool, green-blue sky, but above that a torn selvage of cloud writhed, and vast continents of them were flocking from the north-west. Drops fell heavily on the backs of Richard Milne's hands as he worked.

All at once he was aware of little Johnnie beside him. The child's dark eyes were full and glowing, his dirty face ecstatic, as he gambolled over the sheaves, apparently without seeing Milne, who nevertheless had an attraction which he could not resist. He paused, looking on, the toes of one foot rubbing his calf.

"Where do you come from?"

"Me? Anywhere! Can't I go some!" The boy's bare legs twinkled as he ran, and looked back. "It's going to storm! It's going to storm! But not to-day."

"How do you know not to-day, old man? Don't those stubbles and thistles hurt your feet?"

Stopping at the edge of the uncut oats, the little boy pulled stalks from the wet earth and flung them, roots up, into the air, his bright face turned up until they fell, twisted by the wind.

"I can't help you, so I think I'll go," sang the urchin.

"That's right," agreed Milne, "better go to the house and keep in the dry." But Johnnie stayed, now following behind, now running ahead into the standing oats and out again, stopping, swaying, his face uplifted to the wonder of the sky.

"It don't look like rain, but the drops are falling, falling like spiders."

Richard Milne started, as though he had forgotten something, but he had only remembered, as one to whom every word of magic unlocked a certain door; and he went on with the abandon of one who had longed in idleness for the day of labour. The sweat was in his eyes.

At the end of the field a wide strip of rows of bundles awaited his completion of the round; and as he set up each row evenly a strip was left behind him again, to be widened as the binder made its circuits, until once more he would be faced with a wide expanse of prostrate sheaves in waves. . . .

Johnnie had gone, and there were no more shouts at the horses, nor the shuttling rattle of the binder. Bill Burnstile waved at him from the lane, where he walked behind the three horses to the barn. The long bamboo whip in the derelict binder slenderly speared the uncertain sky. It might be quitting time, though all the afternoon had been dusk. Perhaps Bill was leaving the field in fear of rain, but it was more likely that his horses had had enough for the day.

Instead of looking at his watch, Richard went on working. He was on the side of the forest now, which stirred gustily; and looking toward it, his eye caught the figure of a woman, walking, turning back, going farther within its shade.

After a few steps he was sure, and then he ran.

"Ada! Ada Lethen!"

She stopped and regarded his approach without surprise. Her musical voice greeted him, seeming to change the course of his soul like a rifle bullet in the heart of the hunted. It was a glorious day. But too much of the day's spirit of storm was within him to know the words that he said; and with foreboding he knew only that he was to be drawn into saying all that he ever had said, and as ever vainly. He looked into her quiet face; when her eyes answered his they filled with tears. The two stopped.

"Ada, do you love me?"

"I love you."

THIRTEEN

The words, repeated as though by an echo, left him light-headed; but her lips had moved, she had spoken, at last spoken all. As a crackling fire in a great downpour of rain he was quieted in spirit momentarily even as he held her with fierce arms.

"Then we shall go, Ada. To-day – to-night. Just as we are. We can buy clothes and everything when we get to the city. There is another world besides this one, which you must know. Where you can be all yourself."

As he spoke a doubt like pain spread in his mind, and it was as though she voiced it in her whisper. Everything had been the same before.

"No. No, we cannot go."

Slowly he was numbed, as though he had disenchanted the moment by repetition of an old maleficent charm. Her eyes held his anxiously. In the forest of this world, the same invisible dell of passion and anguish, of a commingled loneliness which made more poignant than all else the solitude of their aching souls. The same; the same!

"We can't."

"Ah, you say that!" he murmured after a moment, in a choking tone. "It's a monstrosity, that feeling. It is as though one in the free air should say, 'I can't breathe,' or an angel, 'I can't fly.' When heaven depends upon it, it suddenly looms as impossible. Oh, Ada, is it your feeling of the oppressive rooms – it must be a long oppression of those rooms of narcissi. It can't be your mind assents to such a lie. . . . Tell me your mind knows that it is only a fallacy."

Ada Lethen glanced aside as though about to walk on; or as though for refuge from inexorable compulsion, from inquiry addressed to her being more poignantly than from the plaintive lips of this man. She raised her slender, large left hand to her breast, in a gesture which tinged for him the bitterness of that moment with the old sense that nothing she could do, no action or tone of hers, but could give inimitable joy, the more profound for seeming to tease with surprise. The trees in a livid frenzy of the wind paused, while a dying breath seemed to brush past the grasses and weeds at their feet. Their silence lasted for a long while, deepened, lapsed, and became stringent again.

"Oh, Richard, I have told you! I have confessed what my whole soul has fought against. And when I tell you I do love you – you are not satisfied."

He stared as though addressing the horizon. "I should be glad you've admitted that you love me, in that case. You are a mystery." But the words of youthful, defiant pique were deepened with a note of restraint from almost maddening uncertainty. She turned away.

As they walked on through the forest its depths grew more profound, more sheltering, though it seemed that they held somewhere a vortex of storm to cover the pair. The tall, stately trunks and thick, fallen trunks, mossy stumps, pools of brown water at the foot of this tree or that, hollows and brush piles, and general unevenness of the ground, made it appear before they had penetrated a hundred yards of the bush that they had traversed miles, over appalling inequalities of footing and divergencies of course. To this effect the obstacles added by raising a resistance in their minds which made them hurry on, hand in hand over the difficult places, until it was as though they were in retreat, a flight whose openness made them a little ashamed to conceal the goal.

"Why must you talk – in this way?" But she gasped as though already they had begun their flight to freedom. She stopped abruptly. They looked at each other.

"Talk!" exclaimed Richard Milne in deepened tones, as it were of wrath. "It is the curse of our whole position." Her eyes fled, remote, but otherwise she did not move by a hair's quivering.

She laughed a little, with a halt, as though from breathlessness or from potential hysteria. "I should have said the lack of talk. My parents do not even discuss each other with me any more."

". . . Give them enough of their accursed silence," muttered the man, as though his thoughts were far away. "Your pity amounts to heartlessness, finally, if it does not lose them their soul." In his mind was a bitter desire to deride their lack of any such possession, to resort to any cruelty, to deny her devotion to them, the devotion which she held so dearly. Shouldn't she suffer for his pain too? What love had those two ever given her? His own detachment – which forced him to restraint and to a realization of the selfishness of which he was a vehicle – won his curses as part of the spell.

As they walked on, the trees thinned on the other side of the bush, and they came to the smooth grass of the border of the woods, the springy, hollow-sounding turf, and walked among the stoic inverted pendulums of the mulleins – frigid northern cactus – under a lowering sky and gusts of wind. From the height of land they could see the river stretched away to the east and below them, like a heavy-linked silver chain extending to the sky, with curves here and there, links formed by a tiny islet, or an overhanging intervened bough. The girl was walking briskly now as though to a definite goal, almost as though she were forgetting him.

"Ada, I don't want you to think I don't appreciate that you love me. Say it again!" Her eyes seemed fixed on some symbolic vision that had nothing to do with the trees, the river, the darkening sky, the drops of heavy rain, the urgent man. "But if you do, there can be no question of things continuing in the manner of the present situation. It's one thing or the other."

The confident words abashed himself, for Ada Lethen was not animated to the length of assent or denial. Her silence made meaningless the most eloquent plea that he could find in his inexhaustible courage to repeat. Before them stood the great beech tree, its upper boughs writhing above the bank of the river; complaining softly, every leaf moved in ecstasy, though the body of the tree itself seemed to be in torment, until they stood above it and looked down into the hollow, to the promontory its roots held against the wear of the river. The curtain of morning-glory vines was spread over the two cedars before it, and on the other side was the curve in the thicketed river bank.

As though remembering that they had stopped, she took one step, and his hand caught her hand, pulling her around. "Let's go down," he said in a tender tone. "Of course we shall." He stepped half sidelong down before her, holding up his palm, which at the last drop, a jump of three feet, she took. Her fingers were not released even when they sat beneath the tree, over the running water, and he held her in his arms. When there was a pause in their kissing he looked down into her eyes, whispering once more, "Say it again."

She bent back her head, looked long with glinting eyes, which seemed to mirror and contain all deviously beautiful and simple things of the world, into his face, and raised her arms to draw his head down.

"I love you."

It was as though the whisper spoken entered, became part of his being, returning between them, until there was no intervention in its passage between her soul and his, his and hers.

With a single movement that seemed familiar, easy as old endearing thought, his arms lifted her. On his knees, her arms never left his neck. They were silent for a long time, until he was again invaded by painful foretaste of the transitory and literal nature, the illusion of possession.

"Why do you feel the way you do?" he muttered hoarsely as if in a fever of haste. "Can't you let those two people take care of themselves? I tell you it would be the best thing that ever happened to them. It would have been the best thing long ago. You see that now? Of course you do!" His arms tightened.

There was a smile on her face he could not see, but her silence was neither indeterminate nor happy. Her cheek touching his drew away as if with resolve. Her voice was almost tearful, "Oh, dear Richard, why must we never forget them? Why must you always try to make me change my mind? You can see my duty as well as I. . . ."

"You see," he returned simply. "Even you want to forget,

you're admitting. . . . You know that you can't be happy that way, and that there must be a change."

All pain seemed focussed in her great steady eyes looking into the forest, and she spoke at length slowly. "You are right that ten years ago – oh, twenty years ago when that happened and I didn't understand, it would have been the right thing to do. Now, how can I? What can be done? I doubt whether either would recognize the tones of the other's voice. When Mother talks to me it is always when he is away, and she worships the narcissi. When I go outside, Father stops his work and tells me what is on his mind. And I know that if they did not have anyone to tell their troubles to –"

Richard Milne was silent again as she had been, withdrawn, his arms as it were galvanized, staring vindictively into the opposite darkening bank of the river. The consciousness of his complete abstraction reached them both at the same instant and he kissed her once more, automatically, and looked away, his mind engaged intensely in a struggle for relevance. She looked at him and a realization crept over her. At last, drawing an immense breath, he spoke, and his words were alien though not unfamiliar.

"Perhaps you think me harsh. You know them better than I. I have never had any doubt that they are, or were, or should have been fine people. You don't object to my being open? Separately, that is." His voice revealed no humorous intention.

"Why should I object to anything you may say," she murmured with a sort of contrition, almost equivalent to repeating her declaration, as though, now, she were determined somehow to accept his love and his convictions coupled with her devotion to her parents, however troubling these commingled elements (in the calm lake of her being).

Richard Milne saw this, and saw the futility of trying to bring her to a choice – a conscious choice – in which her mind would bear the burden. There would come a time when it would be seen accomplished, without her having known. It was as though independently of volition that his words continued.

"What they have done to you. . . . They have shaped your spirit to what it is, and perhaps – certainly I should be the last to complain. But only the rareness of its tempering has saved it. You have come past pain to sweetness. But you would be happier and we could love each other no less, had you not pitied them – too well. When they were hurt, they put you by, callously; then they discovered your power to assuage, and bent your tender soul to theirs like a splint between their festered wounds."

Very still, she made no answer, the eyes dark in her pale face, as though the words had struck her vitally through a recess in the wilderness which guarded her heart. His voice rose in the old unrewarded eloquence.

"Though it gave you all understanding, it was a weight of pity too cruel for a young soul. Though a tree grow beautiful and strong, wind-shaped on a hill, though your spirit has taken on the colour of poetry, you have known too much sacrifice, and I am trembling for the tragedy you may yet know, my lady."

He was conscious of a futile exaltation of spirit, conscious of his own attempt to move her, and in a maze of words he thought that he descried the loss of their love, now it was recognized, and pictured his own barren assuagement in memory. Even the fact that they had confessed their love would not take away the reservations, would not make any difference in the end. He felt like rising and walking away from the spot, but that would make their memories bitter, when they should be tempered with the melancholy of longing, not of regret.

"Dear, dear, my dearest Richard!" Her voice broke on a sob. "I know it must seem hard. . . . You know the tragedy is not – not all in the future. It hasn't been easy. And I can't imagine what would have happened. . . ."

Silenced, humbled by her strong undeniable feeling which at last answered his and cast aside intellectual reservations, Richard Milne kissed her hands, her neck, as though in adoration of her sacrifice.

"Never in future at all," he murmured as one wilfully disregarding the import of life: struggle, from which Ada Lethen had freed herself momentarily by declaring her love, and back to which he must win, if he were to hold his own love and hers in the inexorable condition of development.

Ada Lethen put her tears by, with a little unhappy laugh. "You know," she began, speaking in another curiously more intimate tone. "Father was so grateful to you for advising him in the trouble about the farm. He said he didn't know what he should have done if you had not stepped into the breach."

"Of course, under the circumstances, there was nothing else to do. One couldn't allow such a thing to take place." Richard was anxious to know precisely the facts of the entanglement, which scarcely had seemed vital before. But he could not ask Ada. With all his resentment against her father, he could not expect her to tell him the truth of the matter, even if she understood. For he was assured that there could not be right only on one side and obliquity on the other. That he had come to dislike Carson Hymerson was perhaps more or less extraneous to the case. And his feeling on the other side was even more mixed.

"I remember," he told Ada Lethen, "how I looked up to your father when I was a boy. There was no other man in the community like him. . . . I suppose really I owe him more on that account than I'll ever know. He did not notice my worship, of course. But at meetings of any kind, or church, I would always pick him out, admiring his fine bearing and his features – I would recognize his erect brown head among any crowd. Your father was handsome then. No wonder you are beautiful."

She had slipped from his arms. "We must be going." He clung to her hand and would have drawn her down beside him, but a glance at her face made him rise. What was it? Mere distrust of his eloquence? Was there a jealousy in her attachment for her parents which made perilous all reference to them, even the most favourable? But he did not need to search his memory to know the outcome to that, and to see danger. She had already turned away and begun climbing up the bank.

Whether the evening were coming early because of the overcast and threatening sky, or whether they had lingered in the ravine more nearly insensible to the passing of time than they knew, it seemed that the end of the day had come. Clouds covered the western sky, but as they walked, in silence, a jagged fissure brightened and widened above the horizon, emitting gold rays as it were indirectly, whether from above it or below did not appear.

The wind had died to a faint flaw of warm breeze here and there in the spaces of the bush and the trees, and as they walked they saw great drops hanging from wild-apple twigs, maple leaves, from drooping sumach, and knew that it must have rained more than they knew in their sheltered oblivion.

"Ada," Richard spoke, "I think you love your parents

with a great love. Perhaps it is that capacity in you which has led me to think of you all these years. I'm not particularly a faithful sort, at bottom."

She took his hand and held it over her heart, with a tremulous laugh. "Oh, my love! You're – you're –"

"I'm what?" he asked, smiling in turn, as though a burden were slipping from him.

"You're so – seeing – feeling."

"Well, perhaps I was wanting you simply to Say It Again." His smile was sudden, boyish, naïve.

She pressed the hand as she let it fall gently. "I love you. I'll never forget that."

They descended into a hollow in the path, over which hung tall sumachs, presenting an unbroken front of screen, a spot familiar to Richard's wanderings. Parting the younger shoots, he drew her by the hand within.

There was space here, colonnades of the tall bare sumach stalks twenty feet high, and an impenetrable roof above. After groping for a few feet over the thick crinkled footing of faded sumach leaves and stems, they came to a knoll above a further ravine again shaded with sumach. The extent of the place was indeterminate, perhaps acres, but only faint and indirect emanations of light spotted its complete shelter.

Breathless, they sat down. "You can tell me better here. Sheltered place . . ." Richard muttered. Ada Lethen said not a word, but seemed to have lost volition and tensity in the completeness of their embrace, the frenzied haste and abandon of clinging. And interlocked wholly, it was as though that still muffled soft nook were a temple revealing a mystery even there too plangent and too overwhelming in colour, in the wild clash and fusion of the senses through an ecstasy which they created only to find it again in the whole pressure of a suddenly cognizant universe – lost again in rapt, in over-whelming confusion and merging with an element greater than all their minds groping, their dreams mounting, their hearts seeking, had ever foreknown. . . .

Sobs made him raise his head from her breast. Ada Lethen's face was covered by tears through which her eyes looked with strangeness, and her fingers moved in his hair as he sank back.

". . . so – happy." It could scarcely be heard.

"Mine! Mine!"

FOURTEEN

Yet it was complete content that embraced his mind as he lay in his room that night, and the thought which came to him, whether then or through the hours of sleep, was that nothing mattered, that nothing became worth worrying about until one was starved. . . . He knew that he loved Ada Lethen more than he had ever loved her, but his old desperation was a thing of the past. He never had known that life was so simple, that thinking was unnecessary, and happiness sure. His slumber was deep, complete and satisfying rest, and when he rose the mirror told him he was smiling.

But the day brought uncertainties, and from the natural wish to go directly to the Lethen place he allowed himself to be diverted by the normal routine of the day. All the children were down for breakfast, unusually lively, so that their mother and even Bill had to chide them. Bright sunlight entered the dim kitchen and rested upon the breakfast table. The storm had missed them, and the ground would be in better condition. He knew that Bill expected him to continue helping with the oats. Of course a few words of explanation would straighten that out.

But again, would not Ada think that he was attempting to take advantage of her? And that might prove fatal. Or would she expect him . . . be hurt if he did not come? Shouldn't he think, in any case, get the matter straightened out in his mind, devise a certain and summary means of settling everything, finally and felicitously?

In brief, his gingerly mind in the first hour of the morning allowed itself to be abetted by outer circumstances, and he went to the field to resume shocking.

In high spirits, yet with a certain anticipatory fervour, he trudged to the field. The boys chattered around him, ran ahead with the barking dog, or lagged behind. He was breathing the freshness of the morning air, the new warmth after the heavy rains. Already the mud of the lane, still soft, was drier under foot, no longer slippery. He lifted his head to the sky, blue with thronging white clouds.

But as the day passed, and he attacked row after row of sheaves, he learned that he had reckoned without the change which had taken place, without himself. Perhaps he had unknowingly counted upon seeing Ada Lethen again in the woods. But she did not appear. Feverishly he worked through the hours, and it seemed by a most intense concentration of will only that he was enabled to continue work and not, in or out of sight of Burnstile, to climb the fence and go in search of her to her home.

It seemed to be an endless day, and when the end of it came in sight he was the first to leave the field. After changing his clothes, he came down for supper before Burnstile and the boys had come into the house. Not going to the kitchen where the evening meal was waiting, simmering aromatically, he went to the front veranda and sat down. He would not wait long for supper, hungry as he was, but would go soon to the Lethen home.

There was a summer-evening yellow cast to the air, though the sun was still high. It would set rapidly, and more summarily with the days of approaching autumn. But now Richard Milne saw a fulfilment with the guise of significance in the passing of the summer, and even in his preoccupation he looked out with interest and tenderness at the fields and woods he was so soon to leave. At the roadside, half-way between the lawn gate and the farm gate before the barn, lay a patch of smelling white-pink phlox. The boys were coming past it to supper, with their father trudging behind them, instead of using the path on their own land, parallel with the road. An automobile passed the house, slowed as it met them, and stopped beside the man. Supper, Richard noted with impatience, would be postponed by the length of one of those indefinite rural conversations.

While he was considering going away, for to demand supper on such notice without waiting for the others would be an affront, Alice came around the house, preceded by the cat, after which she ran with stiff back and arms, wide-spread fingers, like some silhouetted figure against a stage curtain: evidently in high spirits. Rustling after came her mother. As they chased each other Mrs. Burnstile laughed.

"I'll lay you right down on the ground and take off your shoes and stockings. I will! Mind you – You just wait till you want to wear my shoes and stockings again."

Alice dodged about the lawn and behind the snowball bush. She was taller than her mother, but slender and quicker. Mrs. Burnstile rustled swiftly about, her arms sloping like wings.

There was the sound of the starting car, and they paused to watch its departure.

"Hurry on, Dad; and rescue me!" cried Alice, breathless, in her halting tones. The boys rushed onto the lawn screaming something about Hymerson. Gaunt Bill followed with a wry smile. The younger girls appeared. Richard Milne stepped down from the veranda, momentarily surprising the women.

"Well, what do you think's happened now?" the farmer demanded of him. "Young Eldon going along now, he tells me Carson Hymerson's gone and kicked over the traces."

"How – what – what'd he do?" everyone wanted to know.

"Well, the story is likely to be different with everyone, and you'll hear all sorts of things. But what *he* says is that Carson had a stroke or something, and they took him away. To the asylum he says, but he could easy have got mixed."

"He's crazy, he's loony! Asylum!" shrilled the boys.

"Children, go in and get washed for supper," commanded Burnstile. Offhand as he had seemed, it was evident that he had not heard the news without being impressed.

"I guess there's some truth about it," he answered Milne's silent look of inquiry. "Well, I can't say I'm altogether surprised at him breaking up. He's not been right. But I can't quite see the reason."

"There is one, we may be sure," Milne replied, turning away. "Was Arvin involved in this?"

"Didn't say. Eldon said he flew into a rage about something, and finally they got the police, and it took a bunch of them. . . . It appears he got vi'lent. He kept hollering something about everybody being in a conspiracy against him."

"That seemed to be his delusion when I was there," remarked Milne.

"Yes, he hollers that old Lethen is a 'stumbling block.' 'Stumbling block to his fellow man!' he yells. And Arvin was an ungrateful cub. And you, you was something, what was it now, a meddler. But Arvin, he was the ungrateful cub you couldn't do anything for."

Throughout supper these statements were repeated and amended. Richard scarcely paid them heed, though he registered them in his mind, and put questions. But after a momentary excitement the boys forgot the whole matter, and they were outside before Richard had taken his hat and gone from the house. They were playing at the roadside, about the patch of odorous phlox. In the first tincture of dusk tobacco moths rose from it, and as they rose the boys swatted them with their caps.

"I'll pull his head off and he'll fly in the air," Bill shrieked, looking after the man.

FIFTEEN

At the Lethen house Ada was sitting on the veranda as she had been another night. For a moment, the difference, the change, was all he felt. Then, curiously, his thought turned and again he knew that he was once more uncertain, fearful of defeat. What could happen? His heart began to shake within him. The feeling of one fractional instant that nothing could be the same, was at once controverted by the certainty that everything was as before.

She heard his step and looked up, startled, rose, half-turned as if actually to re-enter the house. He moved swiftly. Her name on his lips, her hands in his brought the old slow wistful smile, and they sat down together.

"Well, have you made or prepared any good-byes?" An awkward lightness came into his tone, and he felt that in pure anxiety he was smiling foolishly. In his heart he was fearful, uncertain, even as he laughed. Was foreboding an inevitable portion of success? "Happiness maketh all men fools," he said.

"Yes." Her hand pressed his. "Yes," she said, "we are happy." Yet there was a reservation more terrible than matter-of-factness in her tone, so that he restrained himself violently from urging her to his purpose. And before he knew, he was doing that very thing.

"Did you hear about Carson Hymerson?" he asked.

"Yes. Very sad. They say he believed that his son and Mrs. Hymerson were leagued against him."

"Oh, Ada, it's sad, very true, but surely that's not the first thing you see in it. Now your father will be in no danger of losing his place, and you and I are free."

"I wonder." She saw the sad and desperate look on his face as she pronounced the words; she drew near. "Oh, don't think that anything can be the same again. I do love you, Richard. But tell me honestly what you think it means."

"I dare say everything about this accursed place means something I've never guessed or suspected," he said coldly. "There'll never be an end to mysteries, and Carson Hymerson probably has a great deal to do with you and me of which I at least am quite unaware."

"Richard, don't talk like that. He had nothing to do with us."

"He seems to have had, to judge by the way you greeted the news. An absurd old man, embittered by a tortured self-importance and nameless pathological disturbances, goes crazy. Sad! Of course it's sad. The world is full of sadness, if you like. We're not likely to forget that too long. But we've got to forget it sometime, if we're not intending to join the other sad people in cells or underground."

"Dear, if you really want to know the reason I was thinking of it at all, it's only that – well – why should I have to tell you this? People say that Mr. Hymerson wanted Arvin to 'go with' me, in hopes of making a match, they say. It may not be true at all. But they say he always has been teasing Arvin about me."

"Not in my presence."

"Not before you, of course, since he knew of your interest. . . . Arvin and I have always been good friends. We see each other two or three times a year."

Richard Milne was confused with astonishment. "What? How's that? Carson wanted you to marry Arvin?"

"People say he did."

"Well, that explains his attitude, partly. He began to lose hope for that scheme, I suppose, and then he thought he'd try to take your father's farm from him."

"It seems so. Your coming probably disturbed him."

"Not so much as it would have done if I had known," Richard returned grimly.

"Don't you think Arvin was wise?" she asked, smiling.

"I don't doubt his sense of the fitness of things. He saw it was a hopeless match, and did not try to do the impossible." Richard was in better humour now.

She was silent, looking as of old across the familiar country. He lit a cigarette, with something approaching equanimity.

"But tell me, honestly, do you think I can leave here?"

"Yes!" he exclaimed impetuously, as though for the first time, without allowing himself space to divide his mind.

"Ada, it's the very thing you must do, the only thing to be done. You've known too much of thinking first of others, of long tragic thoughts, of unselfishness." His discourse seemed commonplace and stale, but he kept on.

"Look here. I see you in exquisite gowns, radiant, differently beautiful, flattered by the lights of famous restaurants, of ballrooms I know. That's where we're going, for a little time. Do I think you can go? I think there's nothing else you can do, in sanity and health."

He spoke at length and with enthusiasm of his haunts, and possible haunts in the city, and of his friends; spoke with humour, emotion, automatically rising spirits, and enjoyment in courtship which he had never known before. And as the evening passed she turned now and then to look with a smile into his always present eyes, or looked away into those fields and bush she always had known, and which she saw, he was convinced, with the insight lent by the seers and poets of the ages, part and portion in her unique and rich spirit. He had a sense of her opulence such as he had never known before. They talked, were silent, and she was charmed to be charmed. It seemed that they had never before known peace; but it was a fleeting vision. . . . She was sobbing against him. He could not remember any cause in his own words.

"I can't, I can't! Don't you see – what I'm afraid of? The same thing would happen as – Oh, no – nobody knows what would happen."

He was silent. The blow was overwhelming, seemed final, though he seemed always to have expected it. He had found an incontrovertible obstacle. "They're, they're tough!" he brought out with savage absurdity. "I guess if all these years they have managed to stand it, they won't come to any harm. You know what I think – that even yet they would discover each other. Unless you are positive that it is the wrong time, I think it would be well to see them, say to-night, and explain the whole matter to them, get it all straightened out reasonably."

She shuddered.

"You think it wouldn't help? Perhaps it would make things worse. But it seems to be practicable. In fact it seems the only thing to do. If one had a Shakespearean imagination now, to devise some *Measure for Measure* plot, to reconcile them. . . . Alas, such things are too problematical in real life."

Her look was strained, agonized. "I can't think of Mother here alone when I'm gone."

For the first time the thought came to him that if all intervention proved vain, perhaps he would take Mrs. Lethen with them. To his mood even that was not insuperable. Ada and he were going away, whatever the barriers or impedimenta. But he rushed on in urgent words. "Listen. You love me. . . . I love you. We've – we must have each other. Isn't that right?" Her hands and her lips assented. "And we can't be happy here. You see that. I doubt whether I could even attempt to go on with my work. And you must, you *must* get away." He knew that his work, which had been inspired first by her, would never loosen its hold upon him, so that he could not be happy even with her, without it. The realization was confusing, almost sickening.

Was Ada thinking this? She had been looking at him with starry eyes in the pearl dusk. Did she think his decision mere complacent briskness? Now wearily she rose from the bench, and he with her, and before she could turn into the house, he led her half by force down the veranda and they walked in silence about the lawn in the shadow of the tall pines, the upper boughs of which tossed a little in spite of the apparent calm of the evening.

"Let us walk along the river," he proposed at length, when they came to the gate at the road. She shook her head as it were sadly. "Yes," he insisted, pulling her hand. It became limp, as though all animation had gone out of her. He was struck by the difference, perhaps not incongruous, between her attitude and his own inclination to pick her up in his arms and run. Slowly, silently they walked to the veranda.

But they agreed tacitly not to ascend to it, and turned

away to the shadowed lawn once more. There was the feeling that all this had happened before, drearily, many times. They could never do more than return into that house, into the past; and a recognition, a far-off salutation of it would be their only approximation to mortal felicity.

"You don't really believe in happiness, that's it," he pronounced with a slow bitterness as they turned at the gate once more. "You don't believe that we could be happy. Do you?"

Ada Lethen did not answer. Then, as they turned and came beneath a low-sweeping pine-bough, she stopped and her raised arms encircled his neck, and her great eyes looked up . . .

Blood, spirit, pounded through him. They held each other so. The resolve rose in him, lifted him as though on a wave: man or devil, nothing human or enchanted would part them. They'd go. . . . Yet he saw that after all the moment was not yet.

Back on the veranda again they sat clasped, whispering. Darkness had fallen, and with it the breeze had freshened. "You do believe we'll be happy," he muttered softly in her ear. Once more they were beyond time and space. He thought that he detected a movement of assent.

"Above pity, we're above despair," she whispered. Then he knew that her face was wet with tears, and held her close, comforting, though he knew too that they were tears of pure joy. They were no longer hungry and alone, and yet there was nothing left of the world, of life.

Suddenly, he knew not after how long a time, Ada thrust his arms from her, sat back on the bench, looking into the window which gave off the veranda with widening eyes. Without a word or question, quickly he turned, hearing a noise within the room, though doors and windows were closed. But it was too late to see what had happened. The man was there, her father, stooping to the floor. He had somehow dragged the chenille cloth from the table on which the narcissi had been sitting. It must have been by accident, for he was stooped over them, his grey head shaking as with palsy. He straightened one flower and then another, which was ruined. He held them in his hand a moment, looking at them.

Then all at once, as with an access of rage, or in some perverse fear of leaving the thing incomplete, he stamped on the bulbs and slender blossoms, ground them into the carpet. He went to others on the sewing-machine, destroyed those, dashed them to the floor. The two outside could hear his pantings. Ada Lethen's hand became cold, and glancing at her, Richard feared that she would faint.

The crack of light beneath the door facing them widened, the door opened, and at that moment Mrs. Lethen, tall, pale, in white, entered. For an instant, a long moment, her face was like a mask. Then it was seemingly contorted in rage. The man stood with his back to them, at bay.

"I did it!" they heard him hoarsely shout. "I did it purposely. Now what?" He folded his arms with bravado, plainly meaning to insist on his intention.

The livid face of Mrs. Lethen changed. They did not know what to think. It was fright, they knew, white fright in the realization that after all it did not matter, her devotion of years, not in the sudden discovery of feeling, words directed to her from this man. They could see the strength leaving her as she sank into a chair. They thought that she might have come to the time of her death.

The man was still looking at her, changed now insensibly to a culprit air, pathetically ridiculous.

Staring at him, the woman began to laugh, weakly, uncontrollably, laughing hysterically and exhaustingly.

"What a – what a fright! You gave me!" She gasped. "Oh, Frank!"

Mr. Lethen straightened and walked to his wife's chair.

How the other two got away from the veranda, and whether they did so without Ada's parents hearing, they never knew. But they were far down the windy road before Richard Milne could say:

"And now, will you believe me?"

"Foolish boy! When you're right."

Her generous eyes were the stars of that night.

THE END

Northwood, Ontario, Oct.–Dec. 1925.
Hanlan's Point, June–Aug. 1927.

AFTERWORD

One day in 1925, when I was in my second year at law school and my stories had begun to appear in the avant-garde literary magazines in Paris, I saw the name of another Canadian story-teller, Raymond Knister, in one of those magazines. Astonished, I sat down and read the story. And in that same issue this Knister also had a sheaf of farm poems. I liked the farm poems. I could also smell the farm in them. They were simple and direct. They were effortlessly authentic. The story had some of the same quality. I could see that this Knister had the honest eye and neat skill to get down precisely what his eye caught. This remarkable gift didn't quite work for me in the story because without the rhythmic flow of the poems the meticulous observations seemed a trifle laboured. I sat up and took notice because here was a writer from this neck of the woods who aspired to be first-rate.

I suppose Knister was as curious about me as I was about him, for, about a month after I read him, he came to see me. He walked in on me, saying simply, "I'm Raymond Knister," and smiling as if he fully expected I would know all about him. He was of medium height with a very high forehead, a nice looking man a few years older than I, a man with a stutter he tried to control by talking in a sing-song tone. Welcoming him like a long lost brother, I wanted to know where he was from and how it came about that he was appearing in such an international magazine. He was from a farming family, he said. He could not explain how it was that a boy from a farming family, who had spent a little time at Victoria College in Toronto, should have an innate taste for the best in literature. In 1923 he had gone off for a year to Iowa City to serve on the editorial board of *The Midland*, which was certainly one of the best little literary magazines in America. In the summer of 1924, he told me, he lived in Chicago, writing during the day and driving a taxi at night. Musing, I said he must have come from a very cultured farming family. No, he didn't think so, he said, smiling. He was the only one who had a literary talent. Then, as young writers do, getting the feel of each other, we talked about the writers we loved, found some splendid agreements and new excitements. He had read all of Sherwood Anderson, Virginia Woolf, Katherine Mansfield, Dorothy Richardson, Joyce's *Dubliners*, and Turgenev. He loved Turgenev. Well, I parted with him reluctantly and was sure I had found a treasure.

The next time he came to see me, he brought a copy of the issue of *The Midland* that contained his story, "Mist-Green Oats." I really liked this story. It had, of course, that splendid authenticity of all his farm work, but it was brought close to me by a lyric prose flow.

I had introduced Raymond to Loretto, whom I was to marry, and I remember one charming evening in the summer when the three of us walked all the way out to Sunnyside, walking slowly and exchanging profound insights into the other contemporary writers we thought important. Raymond talked about e. e. cummings. Now he declaimed loudly, "When on a pale green gesture of twilight . . ." This was a beautiful poem, he said fervently. He would have liked to have written those lines. He began to talk about his own work. He began to stammer. Then suddenly in a rather loud voice, free from all stammering because he was really singing, he declaimed:

> The trees cry loud, "Oh, who will unchain us!"
>   They gasp crying, but deep mould never stirs.
> Never in this life shall they go whirling: –
>   The storm's great burrs.

Then, laughing, he said, "I wrote that last week and showed it to Charles G.D. Roberts. He told me it was all right except for the last line. What do you think?"

Though I thought of Raymond as a stranger in town, the astonishing thing about him was that he knew all the local literati. At that time I knew none of them. He knew E.J. Pratt, Wilson Macdonald, Roberts, and Mazo de la Roche, who at that time lived with her cousin on Yorkville Avenue and was as poor as a church mouse. Obviously, he wasn't at all shy. I found he simply presented himself to anyone he really wanted to meet.

My own private world, which at that time was in Paris, was widening quickly. All those experimental magazines now wanted stories from me. I wondered if Raymond was getting left out. At the time I owed Hemingway a letter, and when I wrote him, I asked, "By the way, did you notice in that second issue of *This Quarter* the work of another Canadian, Raymond Knister? I know him. What about him?" In a month or so

Hemingway answered my letter but did not mention Raymond Knister.

Before he met me, Raymond had written some pieces for the *Toronto Star Weekly*. The bit of money he got from those pieces had been important to him, he told me. Now he found that this market was drying up for him. I introduced him to the *Weekly* writer, Greg Clarke, who could tell him what the *Weekly* wanted from him. Their meeting wasn't fruitful. Raymond's luck seemed to have run out. "The *Weekly*!" I remember him saying with exasperation, "If they will only tell me exactly how they want it written, I can write it exactly that way." And he actually believed this. Not only was he wrong about this, he was wrong-headed about himself and foolishly stubborn in believing he could make any style his own. He could only be Raymond. He wasn't a hack. Yet he had this strange stubborn faith in himself – a writer with a hundred arrows in his bow. It was this stubbornness at the time which made him so remarkable in this country. He really believed that he could support himself writing uncommercial stories, and not only himself, for he was planning to get married.

I learned myself how annoyingly stubborn Raymond could be. A new issue of *This Quarter* had come out, featuring a story of mine and using nothing of Raymond's. He came to see me and told me that *This Quarter* hadn't paid him for the prose and poetry they had used in their previous issue. I remember how he kept looking at me strangely as he told me this. What happened to that payment?, he wanted to know, waiting grimly for my comment. Well, I knew he needed money, but I didn't know what was on his mind till a week later when he asked me point-blank if they hadn't sent this money to me, believing I would give it to him. I was astonished. A few days later he confronted me again. "Had the money come to me?" he asked. I shouted at him, "Why the hell should they send your money to me? How can you be so stubborn?" Yet I wasn't angry. He was the isolated writer, the hard-up lonely writer grimly determined that his talent should be rewarded by someone somewhere, even if the someone had to be me.

Raymond had also been working on an anthology of Canadian short stories for Macmillan, and that book shows how lovingly he combed the country for any writer who had distinction in the writing of short fiction. *Canadian Short Stories*, published in August 1928, stands out now as a pillar of the times in Canadian writing.

By 1928, knowing I had a novel and a book of stories published in New York, and having finished law school, I got married and went to Paris. For over a year I saw nothing of Raymond. When I returned to Canada, the depression had begun. Those were hard and terrible times for writers. Many stopped writing. I can't remember seeing Raymond for two or three years. I heard that he had gone to Montreal, married, and now had a daughter. I couldn't imagine how he could be earning a living, although he had written his novel *White Narcissus*, which Pelham Edgar had praised highly. And Edgar was right. It is indeed a remarkable book, remarkable in that it seems to demonstrate so perfectly the aspects of Knister's talent that were so strong. The book is a kind of *The Return of the Native* book. A young man returns to his native hearth, the family farm, and the life he had lived there. The woman he was to love is there too. It is the Knister stuff, the real Knister stuff, and here he reveals all his power to create a farm atmosphere and do it all so effortlessly that we never think, here is a writer deliberately creating atmosphere. The smell, the feel, the taste of farm things is in his own bones, and so he works this farm spell on the head.

I saw Raymond for the last time one afternoon in Toronto when he dropped in at my place on Avenue Road and stayed a few hours. He looked very much like himself. He talked about the Montreal literati. Apparently he had met them all. Then he sat down and read a story of mine that was in the *New Yorker*. Smiling, he said enigmatically, "You're now like the ancient mariner." Instead of exploring that one, I asked him how he planned to live now, and he told me that his friend Pelham Edgar had a friend who owned a nice cottage at Port Hope and Edgar had arranged for him to live there. Right now he was trying to finish a story titled "Peaches, Peaches." He wanted to enter the story in a big contest being staged by an American magazine. There was $10,000 in it for the winner. I wished him luck.

Later on he sent me a copy of "Peaches, Peaches," which he had worked on feverishly to get it in to the magazine just under the wire. His wife, he said, had worked just as hard as he had, copying the manuscript. They had high hopes. I read the manuscript. It was full of good work and wonderfully authentic, and yet it was weak in narrative power. I couldn't bear to tell this to him when he still had such high hopes.

A little later, at his uncle's cottage at Stoney Point on Lake St. Clair, Raymond went swimming by himself and drowned.

BY RAYMOND KNISTER

FICTION
White Narcissus (1929)
My Star Predominant (1934)
Selected Stories of Raymond Knister
[ed. Michael Gnarowski] (1972)
The First Day of Spring: Stories and Other Prose
[ed. Peter Stevens] (1976)

POETRY
Collected Poems of Raymond Knister
[ed. Dorothy Livesay] (1949)
Windfalls for Cider: The Poems of Raymond Knister
[ed. Joy Kuropatwa] (1983)

SELECTED WRITINGS
Raymond Knister: Poems, Stories and Essays
[ed. David Arnason] (1975)